When a troubled young man, Ungara, goes on a killing spree in Arnhem Land, the elders contract Kangi, a Kurdaitchii man, to hunt the fugitive down.

Meanwhile, hot on his tracks are Northern Territory police sergeant Ken Wilson and Indigenous policeman Toby Cahill. In the wilderness of the Stone Country they join forces with the Kurdaitchii Man, but Ungara proves to be a hard man to catch. He leads them a merry chase through crocodile-infested swamps, across fire-blackened plains and through tall woodlands.

Just as the northwest monsoon arrives, Ungara leads the hunters into the void of the Goyder River swamps, where the chase will reach a terrifying climax.

Also by Dick Eussen

Australia's Gulf Country
Fishing Kakadu National Park
Duck Hunting Australia
Barramundi and Tropical Freshwater Fishes
Complete Book of Barramundi Fishing
The Savannah Way – Cairns to Broome
The Fishing and Camping Guide to the Top End

Stone Country Justice

DICK EUSSEN

First edition published 2020 by Stories of Oz Publishing
PO Box K57
Haymarket NSW 1240
ABN: 0920230558
facebook.com/storiesofoz
ozbookstore.com

ISBN: 9780648733898
Cover design: James Barron
Cover photograph: Dick Eussen
Typeset in Bembo and Leitura

To all my good mates – enjoy the read and share the adventure.

FOREWORD

This is a fictional story set in Arnhem Land, a remote and isolated region in the Top End of the Northern Territory. Aboriginal culture is alive and thriving there, with many people living on 'homelands' far removed from the few communities that are scattered about this vast 97,000 km^2 region. It has a population of about 12,000 Indigenous people.

Unlike elsewhere in Australia, Arnhem Land was never 'conquered' by invading settlers. Indigenous groups were hostile, killing their stock and some settlers, while punitive police expeditions were driven out by painted warriors.

The first contact with outsiders were the Macassan trepang fishers from the Indonesian island of Celebes. These Muslims sailed to the northern Australian coasts from 1700 onwards until the early 1900s when they were replaced by Japanese pearl divers.

The Macassans had a huge influence on the people of Arnhem Land. Some coastal tribes warred with them, while others befriended them. Macassan men married local women and local men sailed north and married women from the Celebes.

English settlements on Melville Island and the Cobourg Peninsula in the 1800s were short lived, though their influence was huge. Later attempts were made to take up land on the Arufura Swamps, but the settlers were driven out. Unlike the Macassans, the Japanese pearl divers were not so welcome and were fair game for the long spears. The same applied to whites.

I first visited Arnhem Land in 1975 when my wife Eileen and I camped on Malay Bay and later holidayed with friends employed at Beswick. We made annual trips from our Mount Isa home until I gained employment as Information Officer with the Ranger Mine at Jabiru in 1979 and lived there for ten years.

I made friends with a short but muscular man at Beswick while swimming at a Beswick Falls. I was told that he was a Kurdaitchii Man, and a 'witch doctor' by another man. But he stressed the point that he was also a healer and a powerful medicine man who had great knowledge of local healing plants used for various ailments.

The role of the Kurdaitchii Man is not clear cut. It appears to be a universal name in the tropics, though in Central Australia he is called

Kurdaitcha. Elsewhere he is known as Gadaidja, Cadiche, Kadatcha, or Karadji. He is also associated with the ritual known as 'bone pointing'.

When on a mission the Kurdaitchii man leaves no tracks, the reason being that he wears a type of moccasin made from emu feathers, possum skin, and sometimes human hair. Police trackers have refused to track alleged murders after finding an emu feather or fur.

Reportedly, his role in Central Australia is to avenge the dead, but in Arnhem Land and elsewhere in the tropics, his role appears to be more of what the white settlers called a witch doctor or a medicine man.

In his book 'Whispering Wind', Arnhem Land Patrol Officer, Syd Kyle-Little, reported in 1946 that a medicine man, Mahrdei, swam with crocodiles during a ceremony on the Cadell River. Kyle-Little had two 'trackers', brothers Johnny and Oondabund, who lived at Juba Point on Boucat Bay, near present day Maningrida.

I got to know both very well when I lived at Jabiru and often fished the Liverpool River at Maningrida. I asked them about Mahrdei. They told me that he was a very powerful medicine man, a legend in Arnhem Land, and that he did indeed swim with crocodiles during annual corrobboree festivals on the Cadell River until his death. No one else ever took up that part of his career.

They also said that the Kurdaitchii man only killed when he was instructed to do so by a council of elders. He could use any method that suited him: spearing, bone pointing, or a waddy. They said that most were very smart and had great knowledge of healing plants that they shared with some women. But when I asked more, they shrugged their shoulders and said that it was secret 'blackfella' business and that Balanders would not understand.

Balander is a Malay word meaning white man and is widely used in Arnhem Land today.

Part of my job at Jabiru was organising accommodation for staff. Jabiru at the time consisted of a small construction township called Jabiru East. When the main town of Jabiru was built and occupied, Jabiru East was demolished.

One morning I noted a tall, stringy-looking fellow, wearing only a pair of pants and carrying a handful of spears and a womera, walking near the end of the airstrip. Two women and several kids followed a respectful distance behind him, carrying a few belongings.

I pulled up alongside him and said, 'G'day mate, how are you?' But all I got was a baleful glare and he kept on walking. I called the security gate on the UHF radio and asked if they knew anything about the new arrivals. They did not.

I said to leave it to me and that I would take care of the matter. I dropped into the site office and told the manager, Allan McIntosh, about the family. As was his habit he was smoking a curved pipe.

Both Allan and I were appointed Justices of the Peace and often sat in judgement in the Jabiru Magistrate Court. We shared a lot of common interests.

'Bloody hell,' he swore.

'Who is he?' I asked.

'Kurdaitchii Man,' he said.

I never forgot it.

1
CROCODILE ATTACK

From the relative coolness of his air-conditioned office, Northern Territory Police Sergeant Ken Wilson looked through the dusty window across to the distant hills beyond the flood plain. Though it was still early in the day, cattle and horses were already moving off the plain in search of shade, their legs elongated by a rising mirage. Low clouds obscured the northern horizon, the remnants of a big storm that had moaned with thunder during the night when the sky had resembled distance artillery fire. But the storm had collapsed before it reached Balanya. It had only succeeded in increasing the already extreme humidity, an indication that the Wet was coming.

The phone rang; it startled Ken in its suddenness, his mind having wandered out on the plain and the wild monsoon forests beyond it.

'Hello, Balanya Police. Ken speaking, can I

help you?'

'G'day Ken, it's Peter. There's been a fatal crocodile attack upstream from Cahill's Crossing. I need you to take charge of the body recovery operation and remove the croc if possible. Kakadu Rangers will assist and are providing their boat. I only have a raw recruit to spare – that's why I want you to do it. I'll send him over, just in case you need an extra hand.'

Inspector Peter Fields was based at Jabiru and someone not to be trifled with. When he said jump, his officers did.

'Yes sir,' Ken replied. 'I'll take Toby Cahill with me. What he doesn't know about the river and crocodiles isn't worth knowing. Any idea what happened? We've had no word about it over here.'

'I was only made aware of it about ten minutes ago, Ken. From what I know, it seems a big croc rolled a boat with two fishermen in it at the Rockhole entrance. It was witnessed by another party who pulled the survivor into their boat – they're the ones who alerted us. Look, I'd better go; there's been a road accident, a head-on smash near the Wildman River. From reports no one has lived to tell the tale. Cheers Ken.'

Ken walked to a gun safe and unlocked it. There were rifles and shotguns in the safe, including his own firearms. He selected a police-issue Remington Model 700 .308 Winchester calibre rifle mounted with a 4x12 variable Leopold scope sight, a personal favourite. He pushed four 150-grain soft-point Winchester cartridges into the magazine and filled the stock-sock with another ten.

'That should be enough,' he mused as he pulled his Glock model 27 .40 S&W from its holster, checked the magazine, and pushed it back. He pulled a small backpack from a shelf and put a couple of bottles of water and a sat phone in it before heading to the main office.

Constable Sue Raines was in reception when Ken walked in. 'We've had a crocodile attack near the Rockhole, Sue. It appears that someone has become croc poo. I'm taking Toby with me, so you're in charge until I get back. Call Jack and tell him he's on standby just in case something happens. Bill, Harry, and Julie aren't back from their patrol yet. They called in last night saying that they might be delayed because they heard on the bush telegraph that someone is causing trouble at Bowerbird Creek outstation. They're checking it out, but I'd wager they're just enjoying the bush.'

Constable Raines watched Ken walk out, carrying the rifle in his right hand, the pack slung across his left shoulder. He was a tall, rawboned, muscular man, walking with long, easy strides. Beneath his uniform Raines noted his biceps and thigh muscles and reminded herself that she was happily married. She thought him to be good looking in a rugged sort of way, with a clean-cut appearance that belied his toughness. His face was well-tanned from a life spent out under the tropical sun. His short-cropped dark brown hair was highlighted by steely grey eyes that could freeze criminals who had faced his wrath.

At only twenty-six years of age, Ken was one of the youngest sergeants in the Northern Territory Police Force. He was a legend amongst his peers: a man born on the plains of the Wildman River, his father a buffalo farmer and safari lodge operator. His mother, a Sydney socialite, had fallen in love with Colin Wilson during a fishing and hunting expedition with her father. Their affair had been like a romance novel – die-hard locals said it would never last, but with four children and now a successful buffalo run backed by a five-star wilderness wildlife lodge to show for it, the rumour mongers had been disappointed.

Compared to urban dwellers, Ken's early life, and that of his siblings, had been far from ordinary. They lived in an open galvanized shed that provided shade and shelter from the weather and little else and sleeping under mosquito nets on iron bunks. Aboriginal children were their playmates. In the wet season they were marooned on their low hill by flood waters that extended to the far horizons. Even their Aboriginal workers and families moved back to their communities in the high country during the Wet.

His mother had taught all the children from both races basic school under a bough shed. When one turned old enough, he or she was sent off to St John's College in Darwin for further education. Ken had been a good scholar and had joined the NT police force as soon as he was old enough. His boisterous, wild, and adventurous life on the buffalo plains of the Wildman River was the only life he knew.

Ken had served long months in Darwin and later Katherine, but he hated the traffic and the crime and had asked for a transfer to a remote bush location, where he soon made a name for himself in keeping the peace. This fact had not escaped his bosses, who awarded him a higher rank each time they had him transferred to yet another trouble spot where alcohol, drugs, and gambling were rife.

Constable Toby Cahill was making a cup of coffee in the rest room. He was one of the four Indigenous police officers and aides that backed up the community force. Toby was only of short stature, his lean muscular body covered in tribal scars from initiation ceremonies. Toby was a maverick. He spoke impeccable English, rather than the Kriol of the local Indigenous people, though he was prone to lapse into the latter at times. He had spent most of his young life in college, followed by two years at Charles Darwin University where he had studied law. But, as he told it, he had gone walkabout one day to return to his own country and never went back to complete his studies. He had joined the police force soon after.

Toby greeted Ken with a grin and offered to make him a coffee.

'Sorry, Toby, no time,' Ken said grimly. 'There's been another fatal crocodile attack, this time near the Rockhole. We need to get there and recover the body before it vanishes into the guts of the croc. The Kakadu rangers are bringing their big croc-catching boat over. Better change into work overalls and get your gear, mate, and we'll go. I'll grab a body bag. We better take our uniforms as well, in case we get covered in croc shit. Don't want to dirty the 4WD with blood and guts.'

A dirty brown tide was coming in when Ken drove across Cahill's Crossing, the water halfway up the tyres of the Toyota Landcruiser wagon. Several crocodiles were hunting the fish that came up with the tide, the concrete causeway being a deadly trap for barramundi and big diamond mullet. Ken honked the horn at a three-metre crocodile that had taken up position on the crossing. It reluctantly gave way.

There were a few people about, mostly Jabiru-based fishermen, as it was already too hot for the average tourist. 'No one's fishing on the crossing,' Toby noted. 'The word must be out about the crocodile attack.'

Ken parked the wagon in one of the bays at the top boat ramp. The two men walked down to the ramp, where someone was attempting to back a five-metre boat into the rising tidal water. A woman was in the boat, yelling at the driver to straighten up each time he jack-knifed the boat trailer. Ken handed his pack and rifle to Toby and walked up alongside the vehicle. He recognised the driver as Dan Eastman, the team leader of the Kakadu Park's crocodile control team.

'G'day, Dan. Having a bit of trouble?'

'Fuck off, copper. Just stay out of the road and let me do my bloody job,' was the aggressive reply from Eastman, a big man who loved his beer and had obviously been having a few before driving out. Ken could smell the stale grog and body odour as he stood near the window.

'Okay, Dan. Enough is enough. Step out of the vehicle; you're in no condition to drive, let alone back a trailer down a ramp.'

Eastman cursed Ken with all the profanities he could think of. Ken pulled the door handle back, opened it and told him to get out. Eastman obliged, switching the engine off and taking a swing at Ken as he did. Ken easily dodged the haymaker, grabbed and turned him, and then shoved the man hard against the vehicle.

'Back off, you idiot, before you get hurt. Any more of this and I'll be forced to arrest and charge you.'

'Fuck you, arsehole,' Eastman yelled as he pushed himself off the vehicle and rushed at Ken.

The policeman grabbed him by the arms and rolled him in a stomach throw that took the wind out of the big man as he crashed onto the bitumen, his back taking the full force of his weight. Ken rolled him over and cuffed him before he could recover.

'That's it, Eastman. Consider yourself under arrest.'

A police paddy wagon drove up. A young, sunburned constable alighted from it and rushed over. 'G'day, Sergeant, looks like you're having some trouble. Can I help?'

'Sure can. Put this bloke in the dog cage and take him to a cell in Jabiru where he can dry out for his own good. When you're done, come back here and wait for us. In the meantime, I have a job to do.'

Ken noted that the other ranger had not left the boat and was sitting on the gunwale looking amused. It was a woman about his own age, her face shaded by a wide-brimmed hat that hid a pair of sunglasses. She clapped her hands.

'Thank you for that, Sergeant,' she said with a smile. 'The last thing I wanted was a drunken slob in a boat chasing a man-eating crocodile. Best you back this thing in and let's get going.'

Ken laughed, jumped in the Toyota, and backed it down. Toby released the winch cable and the boat slipped into the water as he hung onto the rope. The woman started the outboard and waved to him to toss the rope in, then pushed the bow into the ramp. Toby climbed on board as Ken drove the vehicle and trailer into the carpark, parked it, and joined the crew.

'Hi, I'm Linda Jones,' the woman said. 'Welcome aboard – and thank you for saving me from having to put up with that stupid, slobbering drunk.'

Ken shook hands with her, finding a firm grip. 'I'm Ken Wilson, and this is Toby Cahill.'

With the formalities over, she pointed the bow upriver and pushed the throttle down.

The bow rose and they headed upstream, the

wash splashing and rolling onto the banks as it trailed behind them. It took only minutes before the river opened, revealing tall sandstone walls that rose 150 metres above the tree-lined riverbanks. It was hot and humid on the water, the heat trapped in the gorge almost bringing it to boiling point.

'From the reports I have from the sole survivor, the attack happened just ahead of us, near the Rockhole entrance,' Linda informed the men. 'They were trolling a lure about ten metres out from the right bank when the croc attacked from nowhere and tipped their tinny over. One man was picked up by another fishing boat, but his mate didn't make it. The tinny should be around here somewhere.'

Toby pointed to where the bottom of a four-metre boat was lodged under a shady paperbark tree. 'There's the boat,' he said. 'And just past it – you see that bush, about fifty metres upstream? Underneath that, on that sandbar, is the body – or at least what's left of it.'

'Well spotted, mate,' Ken complimented. He looked at the ranger. 'You okay with this?'

'Yes, I am. I've seen dead people before,' Linda said seriously. 'I was a nurse in another life. Let's go and recover the body; this place gives me the creeps. I don't know about you two, but I can smell that bloody crocodile. He's very close.'

She turned the boat toward the body. 'Only the top half left,' Toby said. 'Be careful, Ken, he won't like us stealing his food.'

The bow lodged into the sandy bank. Ken leaned over to grab hold of the body, then suddenly lunged back and swore as the living nightmare of the tropics torpedoed out of the murky tidal water. The crocodile's enormous reptilian body slammed against the boat with a resounding thud, almost tipping it on its side. Linda swore, fighting to right the craft as the crocodile attacked again. It hit the side with a loud crash, trying to slide on board.

But the purpose-built plate boat had been designed for such attacks, and unlike the fishermen's light aluminum tinny, the crocodile failed to tip it over. The reptile fell back in the water before once again slamming its full weight on the hull, its head slipping over the rail. Ken drew the Glock and fired at point blank range, emptying the magazine, the soft-point bullets hitting the saurian's head. But they failed to penetrate the thick skull that protected its brain, only making it angrier. It fell back in preparation for its next assault on the boat and its occupants.

'The rifle, Toby, get the rifle!' Ken cried. But Toby was already alongside him, slamming a round into the chamber. He pushed the barrel almost into the croc's head and fired as it rose from the water. The report was loud in the dense humid air. Blood, brain, and bone splashed over the two men as the crocodile fell back into the murky tidal water, its head scattered by the bullet.

'Good shot, Toby,' Linda praised as she steadied the boat against the bank. 'Quick, Ken – grab that harpoon and spear him, we don't want to lose him.'

Ken grabbed the harpoon shaft and speared it down behind the reptile's head. The harpoon head lodged under the thick skin as Ken grabbed the rope and pulled it tight, the body twisting heavily under the tidal current.

'Rope the head, Toby,' Ken ordered. 'The harpoon won't hold him for long in this current.'

Linda pushed the bow hard up against the bank as Toby looped a rope over the top jaw, then leaped onto the bank and tied the rope onto a large paperbark tree trunk.

'Whoopee,' yelled the ranger at the top of her voice, 'we got him! How bloody good was that?'

2

MURDER AT BOWERBIRD CREEK

With the crocodile secured, the crew recovered the remains of the body – an unpleasant task, but one that had to be done. 'The other half is probably inside the crocodile,' Ken said solemnly. 'We need to recover it to give the family closure. Let's tow him up the sand bar. We can tie a length around that tree and hopefully pull it up with the boat.'

The plan succeeded, though the engine laboured to haul the huge reptile onto the bar. Only when its tail was out of the water did they realize how big it was.

'Must be close to six metres. A real identity croc,' Linda said in awe. 'What a shame it turned into a man eater. Here – grab this tape. I must record all these things.

'Close,' she said as Toby held the tape on the croc's snout. 'It's just on 5.9 metres, as big as they get around here. His black colour indicates that he must have lived most of his life in freshwater, probably a deep pool upstream. Makes you wonder why he decided to come down and attack a boat. Though he could be hungry – see how he's only got a few teeth? Age probably slowed him down for hunting food. Let's get to work.'

The bagging of the half torso had been easy, however recovering the remains from the crocodile was anything but.

It took their combined effort to roll the croc on its side. Ken took a butcher's knife that Linda handed him and sliced the belly open, the gut and stomach spilling into the sand. Next, he cut the stomach lining, gagging at the stench as the innards were exposed. Part of a leg and the rest of the torso, along with some large rocks, slipped from the stomach onto the sand with a splashing, gurgling noise. Ken picked the body parts up and shoved them in the body bag. Linda assisted him without a word of complaint, though Toby kept a discreet distance. His avoidance of the gore was justified in that he was also guarding them against possible attacks from other crocodiles that were swimming about; one about half the size of the one shot laid out on the sand was only about twenty metres away, floating lazily in the water.

'Okay, that's one job done. Now we need to remove the head or souvenir hunters will claim it,' Linda grunted as she helped Ken to lift the body bag into the boat. 'We can leave the rest; the tide will cover it soon and those crocs will eat the body. They're all cannibals.'

With the task completed they headed back to the boat ramp. There were several vehicles at the ramp, including the media. After pulling the boat out of the water, Ken gave a brief interview to a journalist, then loaded the body bag onto the HiLux driven by the constable who had just returned from delivering Eastman to the lockup. He turned to say goodbye to Linda and saw that she had taken off her overalls and was now in her loose-fitting ranger uniform. Ken noted that underneath it was one hell of a good-looking woman – in fact, he mused, a very beautiful one, if she scrubbed up a little.

'Linda, thank you so much for your help. Toby and I couldn't have done it without you. You were amazing.'

'Thanks Ken. I need a coffee fix, want to join me for one at the Border Store? My shout.'

'I thought you'd never ask. We'd be most happy to join you.'

The men removed their bloody overalls, shoved the garments in a plastic bag, and tossed it into the back of the Toyota. Linda was waiting for them at the store.

'Wow, I hardly recognize you blokes in uniform,' she complimented them as they walked inside. 'What a day, huh? I know I won't forget it any time soon.'

She had removed her hat and combed her short brown hair. Ken noted that she had brown eyes, sparkling with laughter and framed by long eyelashes. It was the first time he had seen her without sunglasses. In his busy life, Ken had only been in love once, but the romance never fostered. It had ended after he was posted out to a remote bush community. Bush life was something that most women avoided, and he had kept his distance from romance ever since, but Linda intrigued him. He wanted to know her better. They sipped their coffee, talking about the morning's events. Crocodile attacks, while not uncommon, rarely happened in this part of the Top End, and the fatal attack had shaken everyone to the core.

Ken discovered that Linda lived at the main ranger station, was single, and loved the bush. He invited her to visit Balanya anytime she felt like it.

She promised him she would. They bid goodbye, but when he held out his hand, she brushed it aside and gave him a warm hug that didn't go unnoticed by Toby.

'That woman likes you, Ken,' he said as they crossed the river on a flat tide. 'She's a good one. Maybe you should marry her and make some babies,' he added with a laugh.

Both men noted that the community was strangely somber when they drove in. There was no gaiety, no people walking about, and no groups were gathered under shady places, playing cards, sitting about, talking, or looking out.

'Something is wrong, Ken,' Toby said in a concerned tone. 'Either something's happened while we were away, or they're sorry for that dead bloke and the crocodile. The crocodile could have been a spirit one, you know. I'm feeling it too.'

Constable Raines looked pale and off-colour when the men walked into the office.

'Thank God you're back, Ken. You haven't heard, have you?

'No, what's happened?'

'Bill called in not long ago. He said that everyone at Bowerbird is dead – murdered, all of them!' Raines said, voice trembling slightly. 'Five people in all. A whole family. There's only one survivor, a little girl. God, how could anyone do such an evil thing?'

'Hell,' Ken swore. 'Have you informed Inspector Fields yet?'

'Of course,' she replied, pushing the dread from her face and returning to professionalism. 'A Darwin forensic team is probably already on the scene. They landed at Jabiru and took a helicopter to Bowerbird. The Inspector wants you up there as well; a helicopter should be here for you soon. He said that you should prepare yourself for a few days in the bush and to take Toby with you, as he's the best tracker we have.'

'Looks like there's no rest for the wicked, Toby. You ready to go?'

Ken saw that Toby was almost grey, his hands shaking. He had grabbed a chair and collapsed into it.

'You okay, Toby? You don't look at all well.'

Toby burst into tears. A pitiful mourning noise came from his mouth, his body shaking.

'Ken, that's – that's my family, my sister's family

that lived there. I must go and see that little girl. She's my family now.' He took a deep breath and sat up straight. 'Mah, of course I'll go, Ken, that's my job. But I need to say goodbye to my family first. I'll see you when the helicopter comes in.'

Back in his office, Ken placed the rifle and pistol in the safe after giving both a quick clean and oiling. He cased the Remington, but deliberated a little before picking up a holstered .357 Magnum S&W Model 686 revolver, loading it with 150-grain soft-point bullets and placing it near his backpack with the rifle. He checked that his sat phone battery was fully charged and added it to his field equipment, a pack that consisted of a Personal Location Beacon, GPS, hunting knife, length of rope, fishing line and hooks, plastic bags, the remains of a roll of duct tape, topographic map, a pair of Leupold 10x50 Mojave binoculars, small first aid, insect repellent, Lifestraw and canteen, basic army field rations, and basic personal items.

He had a quick shower and changed into a full camouflage outfit, shorts and a short-sleeved shirt. It wasn't police issue, but sensible bush clothing for the task ahead in the extreme hot weather conditions. After putting his walking boots on and jamming a wide-brimmed Akubra hat on his head, he picked up his gear and bid goodbye to Sue. He gave her orders to contact headquarters in Darwin for extra police in case the locals got out of control in their sorry mode, which often happened when someone departed. Even riots weren't unheard of.

Sue said that no one apart from herself knew about the killings, but everyone in the village was in some state of unease. But she felt sure that once Toby told his three wives, the village would erupt into 'proper sorry business', with lots of bloodletting from self-inflicted wounds to their heads and bodies.

'Beats me how they know, but they do,' Ken replied. 'The bush telegraph might be fiction in the city but here in the bush it's not. I've asked several elders about it and they reckon that the spirits carry messages on the wind.'

The sound of a helicopter's blades grew steadily louder in the air. 'Hello, here comes the chopper. Take care, Sue, and look after this place while I'm away. I have a feeling it's going to be a long trip.'

The helicopter, a Robinson R44, landed in a cloud of dust behind the police station. Toby ran up, wearing no shirt or boots, only a pair of shorts. Ken knew it was his bush 'uniform': his every day off-duty wear, though he now carried a small pack and wore his Glock pistol and a big hunting knife on his hip.

The helicopter lifted into the cloudless blue sky. 'It's going to rain soon,' remarked the pilot, Graham Jenkins. 'There's been some good coastal storms up north in the last few days. What the hell is going on, by the way? Everyone seems to be in a panic today.'

Ken grimly informed him of the crocodile attack and the murders.

'Bloody mango season always happens during the monsoon build-up,' Ken said. 'It drives man and beast mad. People do stupid things every year – though these Bowerbird killings are unprecedented.'

The wide flood plain fell behind them as the chopper climbed to 300 metres to get over the almost vertical wall of the Arnhem Land Escarpment. Beyond the wall lay a maze of deep, forbidden gorges, some that had never seen a human footprint; dark places where thundering wet season waterfalls watered verdant rainforests and held secrets that no white man knew about. This was the stone country, dreaming country that had been created by the serpent in a time long forgotten. There were other beings that had helped to create these wild lands: the freshwater crocodile that lives in the gorge streams, the black wallaroo, rock wallaby, goanna, and others, all direct descendants of dreamtime spirits that once roamed and built the land when they came ashore at Malay Bay to the north.

These were the ancestors of men who had adopted the totem groups and clans – wallaroo, kangaroo, wallaby, emu, dingo, snake, crocodile, goanna, bowerbird, pigeon, and others. The creators also brought order to the clans, strict rules that must be obeyed; but, man being man, rules were often forgotten and broken, despite the knowledge that punishment could be severe, even deadly.

Toby pointed towards a towering rock that rose high above the monsoon forest.

'Wuraka,' he said. 'You white fellas call it Tor Rock. You can just see Malay Bay beyond it. It's where, in the Dreamtime, Imberombera, the earth mother came ashore. She came from a far-off land and walked on the bottom of the sea, her head held high above the waves. The land in the dream-time was flat, dry, and empty. But Imberombera made rivers, billabongs, and hills. She had a wrap of bamboo about her head and a big dilly-bag that was full of seeds. She planted them and trees and grasses grew quickly. She also had animals in her dilly-bag and let them go so that they could live and eat the plants. Her belly was full of many children and she carried more on her wide hips and shoulders as she walked the country. Then a tall man came from the sea at Allukaladi on the Cobourg Peninsula, Wuraka. They met over there, and she wanted that big man to go with her, but he was very tired because his parla – his penis – was big and heavy, and he had to carry it over his shoulder. He decided to camp, and he's still there today. That's his penis sticking up from where he laid down. You can see his body and head to the north.'

'So, what happened to Imberombera?' asked Jenkins.

'Oh, she walked on and turned into a big rock near Nourlangie Rock,' replied Toby. 'She also got tired after making the Alligator and Wildman

Rivers. She left ten children at different places, who each had children of their own, and now form the ten clans of Kakadu and Western Arnhem Land.'

Toby belonged to this wild land; it was his country, but to Ken and the pilot it was a rocky wilderness of outstanding beauty, a place where no tracks went. Bowerbird Creek flowed between two great vertical walls, a verdant valley about two kilometres wide. It ended far to the north where the creek spilled out into open monsoon forest littered with escarpment outliers.

The Bowerbird Clan had lived in this remote valley, away from the world, since the dreamtime. But in more recent times the families had moved to permanent communities at the end of the dry season to see the wet season out. Years ago, a mining company had bull-dozed and blasted a rough track in from the north, via a side gorge. The track distance was four times longer than the actual distance between the community and the outstation.

Ken pointed to two galvanized sheds and some bough shelters where a helicopter and a vehicle were parked. 'Looks like they got an early start,' he remarked as the R44 dropped down into the valley, landing in a huge spiraling dust cloud near the parked helicopter. The men waited for the dust to settle before they alighted.

A police Toyota Troop Carrier was parked under a shady tree away from the two buildings. A tall, slim man in police overalls walked over and shook hands with Ken and Toby. It was Inspector

Peter Fields.

'G'day, Ken. Great work you both did this morning,' he said, though his voice sounded strained. 'It looks like it's going to be one of those days for us. Three people killed in a head-on smash on the Arnhem Highway near the Wildman River, another by a crocodile, and now this. Five people, three of them children, killed by one of their own. Only one person survived – a girl, about eight years old. She got away and hid in the bush. She's over with Julie, one of your police aides, Ken. Hell, I've never seen so many bodies in one day in all my years of service.'

Ken saw that his boss was visibly shaken and almost at breaking point. And who could blame him? He walked to where two forensic scientists were taking photographs and notes. The bodies were already in body bags and had been placed under a bough shed. Ken was glad of that.

'G'day Ken,' greeted a short stocky man, his rugged face framed by a forensic cap. 'It feels like every time we catch up there's death involved. But this is as bad as it gets. This is Constable Abbie Perkins, my assistant.'

Ken shook hands with them both. He had met Doctor Joe Hockey, the well-respected NT chief forensic scientist, on several occasions and got on well with him.

'They were all bludgeoned to death, possibly with an ironwood fighting stick,' Hockey said. 'The men use these short, heavy weapons to settle arguments, though they're rarely used to kill anyone these days.

Everyone, including the children, received a single well-aimed blow to the head, probably while they were asleep. The little girl with Jimmy was lucky to escape. But she says that her older sister Jessie was abducted by the killer.'

Toby had run over and embraced the girl when they had first landed, but he had since vanished. He turned up after the police had loaded the bodies in the vehicle for transport to the morgue.

'Mah,' Toby exclaimed. 'Two set of tracks. One a small man and the other a child. Heading north – that way,' he added with a swing of his arm. 'Maybe half a day ahead of us. If we go now, we might catch up. No good using the helicopter as they'll hear it coming. Let's hope the killer doesn't know about us – he might not be hiding his tracks.'

3

THE STONE COUNTRY

'The killer's name is Ungara. He's a freshwater man from the upper Mann River country,' Fields informed Ken and Toby. 'The girl said that he arrived a while ago and moved in. But he caused a lot of trouble because he wanted to take Jessie, her older sister, as his wife, but her father objected. She told us that there was a big fight last night and everyone got together and chased Ungara into the bush. He must have returned just before daylight when everyone was sound asleep and done this foul deed. She woke up and ran away and hid until the police vehicle turned up.'

Ken told him that he and Toby were ready to take up the tracks of the fugitives. He handed his cased rifle to one of the police officers and told him that he had no need for it and to secure it when they got back to base. He noted that Toby had three short throwing spears in his hands and a woomera, a spear-throwing stick. He had picked the weapons up in the camp, but Ken had taken little note of it. Toby had also handed his sidearm to the officer.

'Why aren't you taking the rifle, Ken?' asked Fields.

'Because it's extra weight to carry and the .357 Magnum will out range any spears that we may encounter. As for Toby, he prefers traditional weapons in the bush.'

'Okay, fair point. I want you to call me at 5:30 pm every day, or whenever you need assistance. I'll have Graham on standby with his helicopter, ready to fly out in an instant. Sergeant Wally Powel should be at Balanya now with extra police – I reckon all hell will break loose when this gets out, especially when the bodies are released for the funerals. There'll be immense sorry business and bloodletting, and, as you know, things may get out of hand. They always do.' He sighed at the thought of possible riots. 'I'll take Julie and the girl with me and drop them off at Balanya. Take care, Ken. Stay safe out there.'

Toby was comforting the little girl, a pretty young thing, her dusty face smeared with dried-up tears. He handed her to Julie, the police aide. 'You take little Mary to my place,' he said. 'She'll live with my family now.'

The two men headed out on their daunting quest of following the tracks of the killer and his captive. He had made no attempt to hide them. 'He thinks no one will find out about this for a long time. Bad luck for him that a police patrol turned up not long after he left,' Ken said. 'By the way – that was a noble thing you did, Toby, taking that little girl into your family and your heart.'

Toby paused and looked at Ken. There were tears in his eyes, tears that spoke of a great sadness within. 'No, Ken, it is my duty. Her mother was my sister. Mary now belongs to my family. That is our culture.'

The grief suddenly overcame him and he sat down on the ground, his body racked with sobs as he poured out the sadness within him. Ken squatted beside him, placing a consoling arm around the shoulders of the crying man.

'I'm so sorry, Toby,' Ken said quietly. 'Go back and take care of your family. I can take Jimmy with me instead. It won't take long to fly him over.'

'Mah,' spat Toby, 'this is payback, Ken. It's my job to chase Ungara down, spear him, and kill him. That is the law, our tribal law. You know that, so don't stand in my way when the time comes.'

'I can't let you kill him in cold blood, Toby. But you know I respect this tribal business, so when the time comes – well, we'll see what happens.'

The two men pushed on deep into the rock-strewn valley, the walls rising high above the monsoon forest. Toby was like a bloodhound, eyes fixed keenly on the ground, looking for any sign: a disturbed leaf or a stone, a broken stick, damaged grass on the sun-backed earth, or a broken spider web. He missed nothing and kept pointing out to Ken where the tracks were.

'He must have seen or heard the helicopters, because he's started hiding the tracks. That will slow us down, though it looks as if he's heading to the north in an almost straight line. It'll be dark soon – he'll pull up to camp, and we've got no choice but to follow suit. I can't see tracks at night.'

Ken noted that it was close to 5:30 pm; he made a quick call to Fields to update him on the day's movements and signed off with a promise to keep him informed. An hour later, with the sun vanishing behind the high western wall, the two men stopped at a small creek pool for the night's camp. Toby speared two sooty grunters, a catfish, and an archer fish. Ken gathered timber and lit a small cooking fire, careful to avoid tell-tale smoke by only using dry wood. He filled their quart pots and boiled the water. When it bubbled, he tossed in a tea bag and removed the pots from the fire. Toby raked the coals out and placed the fish in the hollow before covering them with more coals.

'We won't go hungry tonight,' Toby said as he sipped the sweet hot tea. 'It's going to be a hot night with plenty of mosquitoes – I'd tell you it's time to wipe some Bushman mozzie repellent on, but by the smell of it you've already got it covered. Sometimes you white fellas get it right in the bush.'

'I have, mate. Hell, I'm hungry, those fish smell really nice.'

'Best fish ever, Ken. Better than barramundi, 'ey?'

'You're a handy man with a spear, Toby. How come you took those ones?'

'They were my brother-in-law's spears. He was the best spear maker in Arnhem Land. One of them will end the life of his killer. I owe him that much.'

The men slept on a bed of leaves, their only protection against the ravaging hordes of mosquitoes their mosquito nets.

Ken slept well, only waking once when a dingo howled nearby: a sharp, drawn-out howl that lingered in the night. Its call was answered by another, probably its mate, from a long way upstream. Ken saw that the moon was up, casting a blueish blush over the valley.

Breakfast was the remains of the fish and a sweet cup of tea before they hit the trail, the bush damp from a foggy morning. It made tracking difficult and Toby eventually completely lost the tracks, but the men decided to keep pushing north, knowing there was nowhere else the killer could go. The rising sun lit up the escarpment walls in harsh orange hues, while overhead, light-grey coastal clouds drifted inland before burning up under the onslaught of the hot sun.

It was the smell of smoke that led them to the remnants of a small fire, its coals still hot. They were back on the trail. Two hours later, Toby pointed out a small stick that had moved, leaving a shallow impression in the hard ground.

'There – that is a track. We aren't that far behind them. They must have slept in. I reckon Jessie is slowing him, too. She must be leaving the tracks for us. Poor girl,' he said, tears welling up in his eyes.

The valley was now closing in on them, the sheer vertical walls almost overhead. The canyon was vegetated by tall monsoon forest and patches of rainforests that were scattered about in damp spots along the flowing creek.

Elsewhere there were rocky outliers that rose above the trees, huge boulders and tors of sandstone that held shelters and caves. There was an abundance of wildlife. About the water holes were colourful flocks of Gouldian and long-tailed finches, while Chestnut-breasted manikins watered alongside vociferous honeyeaters and noisy parakeets. They flushed out quail, partridge pigeons, and rock wallabies as they painstakingly tracked their human prey.

'No one will die from hunger in this land, ever,' Ken said as a flock of partridge pigeons suddenly startled them with a hurried rush of whirring wings. 'I've never seen so much wildlife anywhere away from the flood plains.'

'No one has lived in this place for a long time, Ken. This is my dreaming country. My people drifted away from here a hundred years ago when the missionaries came and put up missions and trading posts on the coast. My great grandfather's people lived here. I know some of these places because he told me the stories that belong to him.'

By midday it became too hot to continue; even Toby felt the extreme heat and complained that his feet were cooking. There was no point in pushing on, as heat exhaustion was a real danger. The canyon was now only about a kilometre wide, the heat trapped inside it pressing down on the men.

They sat in the warm waters of the creek, the intrusion resented by curious freshwater crocodiles and tolerated by turtles that showed little fear. By mid-afternoon they were back on the job, slowly picking up tracks from disturbed stones, sticks, and branches.

'Ungara is now trying very hard to hide the tracks,' Toby observed. 'But it's also slowing him down, which works for us. Bloody hot, Ken, but it'll be dark soon, and a little cooler. We need to find a camp for the night.' He looked up at the sky that was still visible between the valley's walls. 'No rain tonight, but maybe tomorrow.'

A sandy beach, fringing a narrow but deep pool, was selected for the night's bivouac. Toby set off to spear fish while Ken gathered firewood before stripping down and plunging into the pool with a splash. It was heaven; the cooling waters were relaxing and soothing to his sun-scorched skin. He washed his clothes and hung them on a branch. They would be dry by morning. Back in the pool, Ken turned on his back in the cool water and looked up the high sheer wall that fringed the flowing creek. The sun was setting, lighting the ochre-coloured sandstone in deep hues of orange and red. It was an incredibly beautiful scene.

Something moved in his peripheral vision. He turned his eyes towards the bank, where a tall, naked, well-built black man stood silhouetted against the failing light. He had a bundle of spears and a woomera in his left hand and a dead rock wallaby in the other.

Ken cursed; he was totally at the mercy of the man. His revolver was on the bank behind the spearman. There was nothing he could do but try and dodge the spear, he thought, as he pushed himself away from the danger.

But the man hunkered down and placed his weapons on the ground. He stood up, holding out the wallaby, and said something in a language that Ken did not understand.

'It's okay, Ken,' Toby said as he stepped out of the scrub behind the man. 'He means us no harm and wants to share his food and our campfire. He is Kangii, a crocodile man of the saltwater people – a magic Kurdaitchii man. I know of him.'

4

THE KURDAITCHII MAN

Ken had heard whispers of Kangii. He was a bush legend, an invisible shadow who left no tracks and who could talk to and swim with crocodiles. Oddly, he had turned up at Balanya some time back and had lived with the locals in the bush. Rumours had it that he was a Kurdaitchii man: a tribal executioner who could go anywhere in his quest to kill anyone that the tribal elders decided should not live if the ancient laws were broken. But as Kangii had not given the police any trouble, they had no interest in him; after all, it was 'blackfella' business and none of theirs, unless he caused trouble. Ritual tribal killings were not uncommon, and many were never investigated by the police, as a cloak of secrecy and culture made it impossible.

Back on the bank, Toby introduced Ken. He held out his hand, but the man brushed it lightly with the back of his right hand and spoke loudly.

'He can't speak English,' Toby said. 'Don't be offended – that is a traditional welcome. We don't shake hands like white fellas do. He's probably never touched a white man before, or even been this close to one. He's a true bushman who has lived in the bush all his life and has true traditional ways. He is a very important man, a Kurdaitchii and a medicine man who swims with crocodiles.'

Kangii was taller than Ken. The raised weals of cicatrices on his body bore the evidence of many tribal ceremonies. His skin had been cut with a stone knife and ashes rubbed into the wounds to raise the flesh and mark the body. His chest, upper arms, and lower buttocks bore the man-making marks. Kangii had a full beard and long untidy hair. He was naked apart from a pubic wallaby skin tassel that hung down from a skin strap tied around his waist. A small stone knife and a string bag were tied there as well. Underneath his dark eyebrows shone yellow eyes, the result of too much sun and exposure to smoky campfires. He had a broad flat nose that had been bored with a pointed kangaroo bone when he was young. He was muscular, lean, and mean, his body speaking of endurance and great strength. Kangii's polished skin was a shiny black. Ken thought that he was the blackest Aboriginal he had ever seen and that he smelled bad, probably from eating goannas and using their oil to keep his skin smooth.

Kangii looked at Ken, his eyes clear and intelligent. Ken thought him to be a very proud man, bordering on arrogance. Kangii spoke for a long time, looking directly at Ken. He could not understand a word, even though Ken spoke the language of the Wildman River people and had a good understanding of the Kakadu tribes' languages, having grown up with Indigenous playmates.

'He says that he is hunting Ungara and has been instructed by the elders to kill him,' Toby interpreted.

'He has been hunting him all dry season after Ungara killed two people, one of them a woman. It happened in a village nearby where Kangii lives in the bush with his wives and children. He heard that Ungara was at Balanya and made his way there. He camped for some weeks on Catfish Billabong waiting for a word. He didn't know that all the time Ungara was at Bowerbird. When he heard about the killings, he set off and just now caught up with us. He wants to help, and does not care who kills him, as long as Ungara is dead. The tribal council has deemed that Ungara can no longer live. Even if you catch and jail him, Ken, someone will kill him in jail. He is a marked man.'

'Tell him that I am here to take Ungara in alive to face the white men's justice. He will be punished for what he did and spend the rest of his life locked up in jail forever.'

The two men talked and laughed. They were looking at Ken who was still naked and letting the air dry him, which was somewhat impossible under the intense humidity. 'What's so funny? Care to let me in on it, Toby?' Ken asked, a little annoyed that he was unable to take part in the conversation.

'He says you have a big cock, and that you are circumcised but don't have ceremonial scars.'

'You tell him that in white fella culture we don't cut the skin,' Ken laughed. 'And thank him for the compliment.'

The men sat naked around the fire, the smells of wallaby and fish making them hungry. They ate in silence, picking at the cooked meat with their fingers. Ken noted that his companions said little. One would speak and there would be a long pause before it was answered by the other. He knew that this was their custom and respected it by not interrupting.

He also sensed that Kangii thought him to be an inferior man, not because he was white, but because he had not taken part in the man-making ceremonies that the tribes practiced. These ceremonies turned boys into men by marking their bodies with ceremonial scars as a badge of courage and honour. Ken shrugged it off; he had encountered this before from some elders who proudly bore their scars like the medals of honour that white soldiers did.

'Ask him if he knows Ungara personally,' Ken asked Toby, taking advantage of a long lull of silence. Tony directed the question at Kangii who, as was the custom, took his time in answering it. He talked at length, looking directly at Ken, and again there was a lull before Toby spoke for him.

'He knows him well, but they are of a different

tribal clan. He says that Ungara is an owl man. He has no fear of the night when the moon is up, unlike everyone else who sleeps and needs light to walk about when it's dark. Kangii says we should sleep softy because when the moon lights up the land Ungara will walk it without fear of the dark. He may even attack and kill us.'

Ken delayed his next question, ensuring that he followed tradition by allowing a suitable period of silence. He looked directly at Kangii.

'How many people has Ungara killed and why is he like that?' Ken asked.

The reply was slow in coming: 'Kangii says that when Ungara was a little boy his mother must have dropped him on his head. That is why he is different to other people. He's sick in the head. Kangii says he has no idea how many people Ungara has killed. He only knows of the two from the village, and the Bowerbird killings.'

Ken, tired from the long day, retired as the two men sat about the campfire speaking in muted voices. A dingo howled in the darkness as the moon rose and lit up the land. Ken slept soundly but woke as soon as the first throaty calls of the blue-wing kookaburras echoed from the cliffs. As the light increased, so did the vociferous voices and calls of a thousand birds welcoming a new day.

Toby, like himself, had slept under his mosquito net, but Kangii was stretched out on the sand close near the ashes of the fire, a coating of stinking goanna fat protecting him from biting nuisances, while a piece of paperbark he had cut from a tree with his axe protected him from the night. Ken, hot and sweaty from the clammy humid night, slipped into the cool waters of the pool. Kangii was stoking up the fire when Ken stepped back onto the sandy beach.

'Good morning, Kangii,' he said. Kangii stood up and looked at him, then replied in length. Ken could not understand it, apart from Balander, the local word for white man.

'He also wishes you a good day and that it may be a very successful hunt,' Toby said from under his mosquito net. 'He says we should eat and get on the tracks.'

Ken noted that the gorge walls were now only 300 metres apart and closing in about them; the only gaps were other gorges that came in from both sides, some with dry creeks, others with running crystal-clear water flowing across fine yellow sand. Bowerbird Creek was now being fed by many springs that gushed forth from the sand, increasing in size at every kilometre, deep pools and lengths of urgent rushing rapids shaded by monsoon rainforest trees and scrubs.

At midday, Kangii pointed to where lazy smoke curled up from the trees about 200 metres ahead of them. The hunting party was instantly alert; the black men silently fitted spears on their woomeras while the white man drew his revolver from its holster. They stalked forward, careful to stay in the shade of the trees as much as possible, silent and wary. Sticks and dry grasses were avoided at all cost as they would snap and crackle.

They were near the source of the smoke when the brush suddenly erupted in front of them.

Spears were lifted into throwing position and the revolver came up to battery, but the weapons were relaxed as a small wallaby rushed out and fled towards the cliff. Toby laughed softly as the men moved on, more alert than ever after their jolt. The fire had long gone out; the smoke was coming from a burning stick. There was no sign of their prey. The man and the girl had left at daylight. Fish bones lay in the ashes, while depressions in the sand indicated where they had slept.

Kangii pointed to the depressions and spoke with anger. 'He says that the girl was raped last night,' Toby translated with great sorrow in his voice. 'The prints tell that she struggled but Ungara was too strong.'

The tracks were fresh. Ungara had made no attempt to hide them, which confused the trackers. Above them the walls had closed in and soon they found themselves in an amphitheater, the creek flowing deep and strong. The only trees that grew in the canyon were fig trees. There was not enough light for others to grow or flourish.

Ahead was a huge wall where the cliffs had folded together. There was no way out; Ungara had outsmarted himself. He was trapped with nowhere to go. The hunters readied spears and bullets as they crept forward, nerves on edge and adrenalin pumping through their veins. Ken noted that he was shaking. He took a deep breath and told himself to calm down.

The tracks were now clearly visible in the damp sand of the creek bed. Ken wondered why the creek still flowed strongly into the gorge and how it got out. 'There must be a tunnel in the cliff,' Ken whispered to Toby. He nodded in reply and pointed to where a misty spray was visible. A burble of noise, like a waterfall, echoed from the cliffs.

Suddenly they stood on an edge looking down into a huge yawning opening where the creek dropped down for about six metres into a giant, roaring, frothy whirlpool. There was no sign of the man or the girl. The tracks ended on the ledge where the creek plunged into the misty hole.

'Bloody mongrel,' Ken cried angrily above the roar of the water. 'He committed suicide and took the girl with her.'

'No, Ken,' Toby yelled. 'That's the doorway to the low country. Watch Kangii.'

Kangii held his spears and throwing stick tightly against him, stepped back a little, and then rushed forward and leapt feet first into the pool. He vanished under the swirling water.

'There's a tunnel, Ken,' Toby said loudly. 'You jump in and the current takes you into the shallow water and out into the open. Don't fight the current, just let it carry you into the shallows.'

'Have you done this before, Toby?'

'Never, but my great grandfather told me about this place. He did it many times. Even the women with babies did it. I'll go now.'

Without another word, Toby clamped his spears in front of his chest, leaped into the maelstrom, and vanished. Ken held back and prepared to jump before remembering that he had electronic equipment and bullets to keep dry. He unpacked his rucksack and placed the phone, PLB, maps, binoculars, revolver, and ammunition into the plastic bags before sealing them with a few wraps of duct tape. He taped the pack about his stomach as tight as he could and shoved his hat into his shirt.

'Fucking hell, I don't like this one bit,' Ken swore loudly. 'The tunnel could be jammed with logs and we will all drown.'

Despite his apprehension, he took a big breath, wrapped his arms about the pack, and jumped. The water engulfed him like an iron hand. He wanted to struggle, but he remembered Toby's instructions – 'don't fight it.'

Ken wanted to breathe; his lungs were bursting when he was suddenly swept to the bottom, onto a sandy bank. He noted there was now a lack of force in the current. Ken stood up, his legs shaking, taking in deep gulps of air. Ahead of him he saw daylight. It filtered into the huge tunnel, providing enough light for Ken to see that he was standing in the shallow water of the now fifteen-metre-wide, but shallow creek. Ken splashed towards the light.

Here, the tunnel had partly collapsed inward, forming a shallow beach and a rocky spill slope.

His two companions were sitting on a rock, laughing with glee at his discomfort.

'Took you a while, Ken,' Toby cheerfully greeted him, a big smile on his face. 'Kangii said that you wouldn't jump because he reckoned your balls aren't big enough. We had a bet. Mah, I won.'

5

THE LOW COUNTRY

'That was the scariest thing I ever did,' Ken said he sat down on a rock alongside the men, feeling weak in his knees.

'First time for me too, Ken, and for Kangii also. But this story has been told forever and it's alive in our tribal lore. The tunnel was made by the rainbow serpent after he made the stone country and wanted to move back onto the plains. He became lost in the wrong gorge and was unable to climb the high walls, so he bored into the cliff and came out like a big worm this side of the escarpment. True story. My people have always used the hole to travel to this side. No harm will come to anyone unless they fight the current or jump in too early when the creek is running high – because then they will be swept over the edge into the crocodile hole below.'

Kangii pointed to where the tracks of the fugitives were clearly visible on the damp sand. The hunters walked up the slope and stood in awe.

Behind them the escarpment wall rose into the blue sky, while below open monsoon woodlands and distant flood plains extended beyond the horizon. Hills and rocky outliers rose above the trees while green patches indicated where the watercourses, swamps and billabongs were.

Ken had flown over this country in planes and helicopters many times, but here, on foot at the base of the cliffs, he discovered a raw wilderness that was not obvious from a plane. On their right the creek cascaded over the rocks into a deep plunge pool below. Extending from it to the north was a huge swamp dotted with paperbark and pandanus trees and perennial billabongs.

Kangii addressed Ken, who wished he knew what the crocodile man was saying. He looked at Toby. 'He's telling you that below us is the crocodile pool and that it will take a day to go around the swamp unless we brave the crocodiles by walking across it. He thinks that Ungara may have done that.'

Ken unpacked his pack, noting that the plastic bags had done their job well and kept everything dry. He took the field glasses out and scanned the country below him. Dozens of big saltwater crocodiles swam about in the pool below or lazed on the banks. In the distance, herds of Asiatic water buffalo were wallowing in the swamp while Banteng cattle and brumbies rested under shady trees. A myriad of waterfowl complemented masses of snow-white egrets that speckled the swamp like snowflakes every time they flew up.

'There's something there, where those birds are flying,' Toby pointed. 'Might be what we're looking for.'

Ken focused on the area and picked out two figures wading in knee-deep water. They were almost on the other side.

'It's Ungara and Jessie,' Ken almost shouted. 'They're only about two kilometres ahead of us. There must be a shallow place where it's possible to cross the swamp.'

He handed the glasses to Toby, who grunted in agreement before passing the instrument to Kangii. He lifted them to his eyes, looked through them, and reared his head back as if a snake had bitten him. He almost dropped the glasses in surprise. Ken noted the look on his face and steadied the binoculars.

'Tell him to look through them slowly and how to focus by turning the little ring on top with his finger. He's never used a pair. It must have scared the crap out of him when the land suddenly reached out to him.'

Kangii followed the instructions and grunted in wonderment at the Balander's magic. He reached out with his left hand as if trying to touch what the powerful magnification had hauled in. Ken directed Kangii to where the fugitives were almost on the bank. He looked hard and swept the glasses across the swamp before handing them back to Ken.

'We go now, and spear that man,' he said to Toby, who interpreted his simple declaration.

The escarpment dropped behind them as they followed the tracks to where they entered the shallow lily-clad swamp.

The fugitives' path was easy to see: a path where the weeds and lily pads had been disturbed. There was no current in the water and the mud had not yet settled.

Kangii pointed and spoke to Toby. 'He says that we may face a crocodile attack because they were disturbed by the others and are now awake. He says we should stick close together and have our weapons ready.'

Kangii led the way, followed by Toby and Ken, his .357 Magnum revolver in his right hand. The latter pair probed any suspicious looking area with their sharp spears. No one spoke; they moved slowly and silently without splashing.

The swamp had dried up in some sections, isolating islands clad with paperbark trees, tall palms, and stands of pandanus palms. Colourful crimson and double-bar finches whistled loudly as if surprised at the hunters. Some had probably never seen humans before.

Kangii paused, his spear suddenly plunging under the water lilies. His aim was true and something big and powerful struggled on the point. Kangii pushed hard and the struggles ceased. He hauled back and lifted a big barramundi from the water.

'For dinner later,' Toby said, letting out his breath. 'I thought it was a crocodile. But he can't kill one of those – it's his totem.'

The men pushed on, following the path of the fugitives. Ahead of them lay clear water, the absence of water lilies and weeds indicating a greater depth. The head of a crocodile suddenly appeared on the other side, only thirty metres away.

Kangii grunted and pointed the reptile out. He held his hand near his waist to indicate the water depth. They waded in, the deeper water cool and welcome, but Ken noted that he wasn't the only one who was sweating.

The crocodile had vanished. Suddenly it appeared in front of Kangii, silent and menacing, baleful eyes staring at the three men who were so close to each other they appeared as one in the reptile's mind. It was a big prey; the crocodile paused, observing. Kangii began to chant in a soft tone, holding his weapons in one hand and the barramundi in the other. Still chanting, he swept the fish back and forth with a slow fluid motion.

The crocodile appeared mesmerized, thought Ken. No – hypnotized. It moved slowly towards Kangii, who gradually moved the tail of the fish in front of him. Kangii stepped forward as the four-metre reptile opened its mouth and he fearlessly pushed the barramundi into it. The jaws clamped shut with an audible thud. The crocodile turned and swam away, the fish in its mouth. Ken and Toby let out deep breaths as they followed Kangii onto dry land.

They sat under a shady banyan tree only a few metres from the water, watching the crocodile roll with its gift before devouring it. Ken was glad for the spell; he felt that he could not have walked a step on his weak knees. He mentioned it to Toby.

'You're not alone, Ken. Kangii is a legend, a man who swims with crocodiles. I have never believed it, but I do now.'

He spoke to Kangii who flashed his white teeth in a big smile. 'He says that he also has shaky legs and needs to rest before we push on,' Toby laughed. 'There goes another legend. He says it's the first time he's actually done that.'

By late afternoon thunder moaned and rumbled over the savannah, the sound rolling across the woodlands before bouncing off the escarpment in an ominous warning. Kangii spoke as he stood up.

'He says we either need to find shelter or spend a miserable wet night under a tree, because he reckons there's a big storm coming,' Toby interpreted.

The men hit out, following the trail. The land was burning under the onslaught of the sun and the heat was so intense that Ken felt his boots were on fire. He marveled at the bare feet of his companions who showed no indication that they even felt the burning earth. He was glad that they were walking in open timber country, instead of rocks or across a dried-up flood plain.

A tall outlier, in all appearance like a gothic castle complete with miniature towers and figurines, rose above the trees ahead. Kangii pointed and spoke in his clear voice.

'That might be a good spot for the night. There

will be caves and shelters in there,' Toby said. 'But he reckons we sneak up first just in case Ungara is there.'

Ken noted that Kangii was taking charge of the hunt. The presence of the Balander was not important, or even needed, in Kangii's thinking. In this country he was the leader. Ken didn't mind – he and Toby were in strange country where they had no right to be, according to the traditions of the tribes, as they had not sought permission. Their passport was Kangii, who would speak for them should the occasion demand it.

The outlier was surrounded by spilled rocks, bigger than most houses. Beyond them were caves and shelters that held rich friezes of rock art, places where the old people had lived, before they had left to seek a new way of life under the protection of the missionaries and a new God.

The tracks of the fugitives led into a big shelter before heading around the tower and moving away into the forest. They followed them for about a kilometre before Kangii pointed back to the shelters and told Toby that it would rain soon. Darkness was settling over the land by the time they reached the tower. They chose an open tunnel-like complex that went deep into the rocks before opening into a large shallow chamber where logs and the remains of dry branches were stacked up. Thick ash was piled near the entrance. Countless mosquitoes welcomed them in a cloud-like formation. Kangii had vanished.

'This was once home to a big family,' Tony said

to Ken. 'Look at the handprints on the wall from the children when they had nothing to do. Mah – these bloody mosquitoes, we need to do something about them! Ken, you get firewood and I'll find some soft leaves for beds.'

Ken soon had a pile of timber heaped up as the thunder moaned overhead; the first splatter of rain raised little spurts of dust as it hit the dry cracked ground outside. It was almost dark when Kangii returned, dripping wet from the rain. He tossed a big spotted goanna near the fire that Ken had lit, a big grin on his bearded face.

Toby entered the cave, his arms full of fresh green leaves that he had pulled from nearby scrubs. 'Great, goanna for dinner! It's the best tucker,' he said with joy. 'Now we have to light some little fires and get rid of the mosquitoes.'

The men soon had several small fires going in the chamber and another at the entrance. Some green leaves were tossed onto the flame. A pungent, but not unpleasant, smell permeated the shelter. It made the men cough, but it drove the biting nuisances away.

'No mosquitoes will be in here tonight,' Toby informed Ken. 'You get used to the smell. Better than being eaten alive, I reckon.'

Ken watched as Kangii pushed a slim stick with a knot on its end up the anus of the dead goanna, twisted it several times, and withdrew it.

The reptile's innards came out with it. Kangii placed the goanna belly up on the coals and grunted, happy in his work. Much later he removed the cooked body and cut a slit in the stomach area. The cavity was awash with juices. He sucked on them before passing the goanna to Toby, who did the same before passing it to Ken. Ken sucked out what remained of the tasty soup and handed the reptile back to Kangii, who placed it on a smooth rock and cut away some meat with his stone knife. He handed out the morsels in equal share to the men.

They ate in silence, keeping their thoughts to themselves. Ken had called his boss and informed him that the fugitives had left the stone country and were moving northeast towards the distant coast. The Inspector told him to stay on the tracks and that he would have a patrol from Maningrida try and cut the outlaw off before they reached Ungara's home country. 'There are several homelands and many vehicle tracks in that part of the country, and if we can widen the hunt to force him out, he may make a mistake,' were his parting words.

The men bedded down around the fire; beyond, in the darkness, the dreamtime storm god Namarrkun tossed stone axes at the clouds, setting off sparks and creating the lighting and thunder. Heavy rain poured down, soaking into the thirsty earth. The storm passed as quickly as it had begun, but the tired men did not notice it, or the moon that revealed itself and lit up the bush as the thunder god ran away and vanished far to the south.

6

ATTACK

Ken was sleeping soundly when a sudden scream startled him into full alertness. There were yells and grunts of struggling men, their forms silhouetted against the light of the moon at the shelter entrance. The fire had long gone out. Ken found his torch that he had placed next to his revolver. He picked both up and switched the torch on, the powerful 400-lumen beam lighting up the scene.

Kangii was struggling with someone while Toby was fighting for his life with a naked man, yelling for help. Ken rushed towards the pair, but the attacker pulled free, turned, and ran away into the tunnel. Ken fired three rapid shots, the concussions inside the cave making his ears ring. He knew that he had missed.

'Don't go after him, Ken,' Toby cried. 'It's Ungara, he can see in the dark. Wait until daylight. He's too fast. The bastard broke my arm.'

Ken turned and shone the torch on Toby. His face was a bloody mess and he was holding his left arm, his body shaking in pain. Kangii was holding a struggling girl. Toby yelled at her loudly, and she instantly stopped struggling and spoke to him in the Gagadju dialect that Ken understood.

'Uncle Toby, is that you?'

'It's me, Jessie. We've come to save you.'

Kangii released her and she rushed to embrace Toby. She cried with loud, body-racking sobs, holding him as tight as she could. Toby cried with her, though Ken could not tell if his tears were of joy or pain; probably both, he reflected. Kangii tossed wood on the dying coals of the campfire. It flared up and lit the shelter.

'Okay, Toby,' Ken said as he leaned alongside him. 'Let me have a look at you. Looks like you copped it really good.'

'I did, Ken. I woke up and started to sit up when he hit me on the head, but he missed most of it. His next blow was on my arm. I felt it snap. I just grabbed the club with my good hand and held on tight.'

It was Jessie who had screamed when Kangii had grabbed her. Ungara had told her that the men who were following them were coming to kill them, the same as they had done to her family. She said that she had been unaware of the slaughter of her family until Ungara had put a hand over her mouth and told her to be silent and to come with him because someone was killing everyone. She had gone along of her own free will, but a day into their flight she had become suspicious and started to leave signs in case someone came looking for her. She broke into tears when she said that she had been raped several times and that Ungara had hit her hard if she did not keep up or obey him.

At the first sign of dawn, a time when the blue-wing kookaburras heralds a new day with raucous calls, Ken walked away from the safety of the cave and rang Inspector Fields on the sat phone. There was some delay before it was answered.

'Ken. Peter here, what happened?'

'We were attacked by Ungara during the night. Toby has a bad head wound and a broken arm. We have Jessie, but she's also in a bad way. Both need medical attention ASAP.'

'Right, Ken, I'll get Graham to pick them up. But what are you going to do, continue the chase?'

'Yes. Kangii will help, but we can't communicate, apart from some sign language. Is it possible to get Constable Jimmy Cooper from Maningrida to join us?'

'Can't see why not, Ken. He knows that country and is one of the best trackers in the business. I'll organize it. What are your coordinates?'

Ken gave the waypoint of his GPS to Fields, who advised him that he would call him back. Kangii was boiling water in the quart pots when Ken returned. The hot sweet tea was welcome, but no one felt like eating. Ken informed Toby that he and Jessie would soon be airlifted out and that police constable and tracker Jimmy Cooper from Maningrida would replace him. He asked him to pass it onto Kangii.

The news appeased Kangii who spoke at length to Toby. 'He says that Jimmy is a good man, a cousin of his. He knows him well and thinks you have made a very good choice, but he is also sorry to lose me and will miss me. We've become good friends during the last few days.'

Fields called back half an hour later. 'Ken, there's a homeland with an airstrip about twenty minutes' walk to the northeast of you – Wurakii. There's no one there at the moment; the police have been busy. Yesterday we evacuated every homeland in the area to make sure Ungara does no more harm. The strip's in good shape. Go there and wait for the plane; it'll have Jimmy on board, as well as some fresh supplies and batteries. The helicopter is also en route and will get to you soon. Call me if you need anything.'

Time passed. The sun came up and heated the land, driving the birds to water and under shelter from its fierce rays. The trees dropped leaves continuously to stay alive in the intense heat. The rain had only been sparse and not enough had fallen to close the cracks in the baked earth. Only the sad cries of the black cockatoos, the cawing of crows, and the clattering of a rock dislodged by a wallaby broke the silence of the bush. There was no wind, no air, only sun.

The sound of the helicopter alerted the hunters. Kangii had wanted to go on alone but had been talked out of it by Toby, who told him that without his guidance the Balander would become lost in the bush and die.

The chopper landed, stirring up a cloud of black dust from the burned grasses under the spinning rotors. Jenkins alighted and shook hands with Ken. He had a passenger with him. Ken was surprised when he saw that it was Linda Jones.

'I thought that you might need a nurse,' Jenkins explained. 'My wife and I are good friends with Linda. She's on her days off and they were both visiting me at Balanya. Linda offered to come along in case she was needed.'

'Hi Ken,' Linda greeted him. 'My, you look wild – and smell like it, too!' she added with a laugh as she hugged him tightly before pushing him away. 'Now where are my patients?'

She thoroughly checked Toby out before looking at Jessie. 'Both need to go to Darwin. Toby needs X-rays and Jessie is suffering from severe exhaustion that will require medical care. She also told me that she's been raped. Let's put them on board. By the time we arrive at Balanya, the Air Ambulance will be on the ground to take them to Darwin.'

Toby insisted that his spears travel with him, as they held memories of his brother-in-law. Ken and Kangii watched in silence as the R44 lifted and headed south. Ken set a direct course for the airstrip. It was mid-morning when they arrived. They checked the building, but apart from dozens of tail-wagging dogs left behind to fend for themselves, there was no one there. Kangii pointed to a set of footprints in the sand. 'Ungara,' he grunted with delight in his voice. He said more but it was lost on Ken.

Ken pulled the topographic map from his pack and opened it. He had marked their route on it since he had left the Bowerbird homeland. Kangii could not read but he had taken a great interest in the map and the GPS and understood both very well. Ken pointed to where they were and said, 'Warakijii.' Kangii nodded and traced his finger across the map until it stopped where a large billabong was marked.

'Binin Anlapalii, Ungara,' he said in his clear voice. He moved his finger north to where the Blyth River entered the Arufura Sea. 'Jii-marajii,' he added, tapping a place name on the map. Kangii pointed at his chest and again at the river region. Ken knew that he was telling him that it was his homeland and country.

They were interrupted by the sound of a single engine plane coming in for a landing. It landed with a thud and several bounces on the rough strip, trailing a plume of dust behind it as it taxied to the galvanized buildings. It turned about, forcing the two men to duck for cover as dust and grit washed over them. A passenger disembarked from it; the plane taxied and took off with a roar of its engine.

Jimmy Cooper was a tall, skinny man who resembled Kangii in looks and manner. He wore a loose-fitting police issue overall, his eyes shaded with a pair of dark glasses that appeared to sit on his full beard. A red cap covered his long untidy hair. He carried a Remington Model 870 pump-action twelve-gauge shotgun, and had a small pack slung across his shoulder and a bag in his hand. He wore a pair of thongs on his feet.

He dropped the bag at Ken's feet and held out his hand. Ken brushed it lightly in the same fashion that the local people did. 'G'day Jimmy, welcome to the bush. I believe you know Kangii.'

'I sure do, Ken,' was his reply as he turned to Kangii with a big smile, speaking to him in their own language. They conversed for a while, totally ignoring Ken, but, knowing their ways, he kept his patience and said nothing. Unlike Toby, Jimmy only spoke Kriol with many Language words tossed into the conversation. He looked at Ken with respect.

'Kangii said you one big tough Balander, as good as any blackfella. He said that Ungara go to Binjii Billabong. Maybe he bin right on that one. Plenty big corroboree tonight when that new moon is full up. All people from all about bin go there.'

'I thought no one was in this part of the country,' Ken said. 'Inspector Fields said that everyone had been moved out because the police reckon that Ungara might kill more people.'

'Mah, no people in the homelands, no more, Ken. But that corroboree big meeting place for many people. Maybe Ungara not go there, too many spears and shotguns,' Jimmy replied, patting the butt of his shotgun.

'But Kangii say that he will because he wants another woman. That boy fuck too much, he wants woman all the time. Police there too, Sergeant Matt Hardin, Constable Wayne Smith, and plenty blackfella police. They look for Ungara and keep all that people safe. I think,' Jimmy added in afterthought, slowly stroking his beard.

'That Ungara moon man, he bin see at night when everyone else sleeps. Kangii says go there now.' Jimmy pointed at the bag. 'Tucker in that tucker bag, and things we want. Plenty water, too; no water in that country. Long way to walk.'

The men sat out, no longer bothering to follow the tracks of the outlaw. It gave them more mobility and hope that they would catch up to him. The forest thinned out, meeting a huge, seemingly endless plain capped by short stunted bushes; the meagre plant life was dwarfed by enormous, sun-scorched magnetic termite mounds that were seemingly suspended above the ground in a shimmering mirage. Oddly, the grass had not been burned. Ken remarked on it, but Jimmy shrugged his shoulders and would not, or could not, comment.

Hours later, they were halfway across the plain when Kangii uttered a curse and pointed ahead, where plumes of smokes suddenly billowed into the air. He spoke in alarm to Jimmy.

'Kangii says that Ungara lit the grass to burn us out and hide his tracks,' Jimmy said.

'He say that fire will overtake us before we can

get away from this place. He say we should backburn or we die. But maybe dry waterhole somewhere. Kangii say you should check GPS, maybe one close up.'

Ken looked at his GPS and pointed to where the map indicated a depression only about a kilometre ahead. Kangii grunted and set off at a loping run, followed by his companions. The horizon ahead was obscured by a dense smoke cloud that spread widely across the plain, the plume rising several hundred metres into the sky. They were only halfway to their destination when the acrid smoke drifted over them, cutting visibility down to only a few metres.

Kangii was well ahead, with Jimmy close on his heels. Ken almost lost sight of the men when they stopped. The crackling of the ten-metre-high flames surrounded them, the flickering light barely visible through the thick smoke. The two indigenous men had stopped in a shallow grassless depression, about fifty metres in circumference: a dried swamp bed. It had long since dried up, but the men hardly noticed it as they fell flat onto their faces in the center, the flames roaring and licking over them. The heat was intense; they couldn't breathe. Ken pulled his shirt off and over his face, rolling across to share it with Kangii, who was coughing and gasping. Long minutes elapsed, the men wheezing, eyes screwed tightly shut, before the flames passed on and left only dense, acrid smoke in their wake.

Ken felt like his back had been badly sunburned when he finally stood up. Rifling through their supplies, he gulped down a long drink from the water bottle before passing it on. The men were covered in soot. Kangii laughed and made a grinning remark.

'He say you all the same as us blackfella now, Ken,' Jimmy grinned. 'You now black like us.'

Ken reported later that the trek across the burned plain was the hardest of the chase they encountered. Their water ran out when they were almost across, and his feet were burning in his boots. It even bothered the Indigenous members of the party, who showed rare signs of discomfort, going so far as to pour precious water on their feet to cool them. Jimmy tossed his thongs away when a strap broke on one during the flight for safety across the plain. 'Bloody blow-out, 'ey,' he swore, a grin on his bearded face.

At last they reached the forest and the Mann River, thankfully still trickling. The men threw themselves into a shallow hole. Ken swore that he saw steam rising from their hot bodies.

7

CROCODILE CORROBOREE

They found the tracks of their prey heading downstream, but lost it in rocky country, where the river cut through low sandstone escarpments and hills.

'We go to Binjii Billabong,' Jimmy said to Ken. 'Ungara will be there for sure. Kangii has big business there. Big corroboree mob there, come from all about this country for crocodile business.'

Ken had heard about the meeting. It was an event that occurred annually and always on the full moon. He had heard rumours about people swimming and riding on the backs of crocodiles, but they were just that – rumours. He looked forward to finding the truth.

A small wallaby broke cover from a pandanus thicket. Kangii speared it before it could take more than a few hops. Ken was impressed; he couldn't draw and fire his revolver any faster or more accurately. Kangii pulled the spear out of the unfortunate animal and picked it up by the tail. He grinned, pleased with the food and spoke to Ken before moving on. Jimmy laughed. 'Tucker for tonight, Ken. He say we starve if not for him.'

The timbered hills fell behind as they entered open forest. They came across a vehicle track and followed it. Suddenly a Toyota trayback loaded with people broke from the trees, headed toward them.

The driver pulled up alongside the group, his face lit up by a big grin. 'Ey, what you blokes doing here?' he yelled in Kriol with a loud voice. 'Ey, Jimmy! It's you, brother, I see you.'

'Nundul, mate, you sight for sore eyes,' shouted Jimmy in a happy tone. 'What you people doing here?'

'We look for annaburoo, but bin scarce. You bin see one up there?'

'Nothing, only wallaby,' Jimmy replied, pointing to Kangii and his successful catch. 'No buffalo, nothing.'

For the first time, Nundul recognised Kangii. His eyes opened wide and he spoke a welcome in the local language, leaving Ken frustrated as to what was said. Others had jumped from the vehicle and were touching Kangii on the shoulder in greeting. It looked as though they were welcoming a king. Kangii was obviously a very important man in this part of the world.

Nundul offered them a lift to the camp which they gladly accepted. Ken felt strange in the back of the vehicle, jammed in by a dozen sweaty and unwashed dust-covered bodies, but he told himself that he probably smelled as bad. Ken was surprised at the number of vehicles – over a hundred, at a glance – and camps scattered in a disorganized manner under the trees on the banks of a huge billabong. Nundul sounded the horn and drove into the camp; he drove slowly, to keep the dust down and to avoid numerous playing kids and mangy camp dogs.

His passengers yelled and called out to others and pointed at Kangii who stood tall and proud above the cabin, his spears in one hand.

When the vehicle came to a stop they were surrounded by a throng of people; men, women, and children alike. They called out repeatedly with cries of joy, chanting, 'Kangii, Kangii, Kangii!'

Ken was left alone in the tray; no one took any notice of him. He felt invisible.

'Ken, is that you? What the hell are you doing here?'

He looked about and came face to face with Inspector Fields and Sergeant Matt Hardin, the officer in charge of the Maningrida district. Ken jumped down and shook hands with the two police officers.

'Fuck, you blokes look good,' Ken said, relief in his voice. 'I wasn't too sure if I would be welcome here with all that blackfella business going on.'

'Under normal circumstance no Balanders would be allowed here at all, Ken,' Hardin said. 'But these are not normal times. We have a killer in the bush, and even with all their numbers they are frightened of what Ungara may do. Plus, there's the fact that if anyone kills him, there will be payback from his family members. Some of these things end in a full-scale war. Only a designated Kurdaitchii man or a white policeman can kill him. That's the law. Who the hell is the tall bloke with the spears you brought in – and where's Jimmy?'

'That was Kangii, the crocodile man and the tribal appointed executioner of Ungara. Jimmy got pulled along with the mob. He should turn up soon. Hell, what is that stink? It smells like rotten fish.'

'It is, Ken,' Hardin, a tall ruddy-faced redheaded man, replied. 'Those early storms generated a bit of flood flow-off into the billabong and muddied it. The barramundis and other fish are dying due to the lack of oxygen and suspended solids that are clogging up their gills. There are heaps of dead fish piled up on the banks and in the water. Let's go to the police camp, you can't smell it from there.'

The men walked to the police camp. It was sited some distance away, under tall trees where a large fly, tied off between tree trunks, shaded chairs and tables. A mobile kitchen, shower tent, and several mosquito dome shelters and swags were scattered about the camp. A generator ran softly in the background. Several police vehicles and a Toyota Troop carrier that had been converted into an ambulance were parked nearby.

'Hell, this is a big camp. How many men have

you got here?' Ken asked.

'Fourteen, including four women police aides, a cook, and two ambulance officers,' Fields replied. 'I have four white police officers – six including you and me. The others are police aides. I flew in an hour ago. It was a spur of the moment thing. We were asked by the elders to provide protection, a rare thing when it comes to blackfella politics in this country. No white man has seen this event since the 1950s, when a patrol officer documented it. It's not so much keeping the peace, more so protecting everyone from Ungara. Now that he doesn't have a woman, everyone feels he will raid the camp to steal a young girl. He will kill anyone who stands in the way. We have patrols out day and night on the camp perimeter.'

Hardin handed Ken an icy-cold Staminade drink from the fridge. 'Here, Ken, get some of this stuff into you. You look like hell. How far have you come today?'

'We got lucky, Jack. But we still trekked for some ten kays over some of the hardest country that I've ever come across. Ungara tried to burn us out and almost succeeded; he sure cooked our feet pretty well. Had it not been for the water that Jimmy brought with him we would've been done in. Our luck held when a hunting party came across us and gave us a lift. We lost Ungara's track a way back, but he's heading here. We probably passed him in the Toyota. No doubt he saw us.'

'Well mate, there's a shower over there, and clean police overalls and towels in that box,' Hatfield said politely. 'You stink, and that is putting it mildly. Here comes Jimmy. I better get him a drink – he loves his lolly water.'

Ken felt reborn after his shower, though the overalls were hot and uncomfortable. Jimmy informed the men that Kangii had taken up residence with some family members in a camp near the water.

He said that a big corroboree in his honour would be held when the moon came up and that Kangii would swim with the crocodiles when the sun went down, something they should not miss.

The men walked down to where hundreds of people were gathering, some squatting, others sitting or standing in the dirt, all looking out over the water. The sun was setting over the billabong, a blood red orb filtered by the smoke of distance bushfires, the reflections resembling a staircase to the sun. Nervous waterfowl swam amongst the lilies, while several big crocodiles floated on the surface of the deeper water. The stench of dead barramundi was overwhelming on the water's edge. Hundreds of carcasses were pushed up against the banks. The crowd was silent; only a low murmur could be heard.

Suddenly a tall man stood up and walked toward the water. It was Kangii. He was totally naked. The crowd was silent; there wasn't even a cough. The children were wide-eyed and clinging to their parents. Kangii started to chant, the sound echoing over the people before fading away across the billabong. Ken recognised it as the same chant

Kangii had sung to the swamp crocodile.

Kangii was now at the water's edge. He pulled a big barramundi from the water, its rotten flesh falling away. Kangii pulled it apart and anointed his whole body with the stinking fish, using the skin like a face cloth. The smell was bad, but no one noticed it, everyone holding a collective breath.

The chant had an almost hypnotic effect on the people; even the Balanders felt the magic of the moment, highlighted and mesmerized by the surreal light of the closing day. Kangii stepped into the shallow water, slapping it slowly with a vibrating motion, creating small bubbles that spread out across the water in front of him, the drone of his voice never stopping.

Suddenly there was a gasp from the audience as a huge crocodile materialized in front of Kangii, its massive body rising slowly from the water.

But Kangii never flinched, the palms of his hands vibrating the water, accompanied by his voice. The crocodile slowly moved forward. Ken drew his revolver, but he was stopped by Hardin, who grabbed him by the arm and held him back.

'No Ken, we don't interfere, no matter what. This is blackfella business.'

Ken pushed the revolver back in its holster as the crocodile nosed up to the vibrating hands before turning and laying side on beside Kangii. His voice never changed as he stepped forward into waist-deep water and touched the crocodile before slowly rubbing its back. There was absolute silence; even the vociferous corellas that were settling into roosts in the trees on the other side of the billabong were hushed.

The sun had set beyond the rim of the trees, leaving an eerie surreal glow in its wake, an almost invisible faint blush of pale pink spreading out across the sky.

Slowly, almost without visible movement, Kangii slipped onto the back of the huge saurian and lay on top of him. It swam into deeper water and dived with a massive surge of its tail. The water closed over the scene. Darkness fell. There was no sight of Kangii; he had vanished with the crocodile into the murky depths. There was a gasp from the crowd, followed by cries of horror and sorrow from the women. Children cried.

'What the hell happened?' Ken asked Jimmy. 'Where is Kangii? Did the croc take him?'

'Kangii not dead, Ken, no way. He back later, all the same as Jesus. He did that many times before,' Jimmy replied. 'That man, he very powerful, he now that crocodile spirit.'

The people were moving away to their camps, talking in low tones about what they had witnessed. The white police walked back, silent and thoughtful about the event.

'Not sure how he does it,' Hardin mused. 'No doubt the crocodiles' bellies are full of dead barramundi and they're sick and tired of it, which is why Kangii anointed himself with the stinking fish. But crocodiles are opportunist hunters, and not being hungry now doesn't mean that they won't kill and save food for later. Kangii took a hell of a risk in doing what he did. He has more guts than anyone I've ever known. But will he be back? That's the real question.'

8

SHADOWS

The cook was busy cooking dinner on a Weber barbeque. Soon, thick steaks were served, plated with baked and green vegetables. The police officers and aides filtered in for the feast and left as soon as they finished. There was a constant movement of people. Ken and Peter were introduced to all of them, including the two Indigenous ambulance officers.

Ken had met one before: Adrian Wilson, who reckoned that Ken was a relative of his as they shared the same name. Ken didn't have the heart to tell him that many Indigenous locals had been named Wilson, or Owen, after being baptized by the Reverend Owen Wilson, who had spent a lifetime doing missionary work in Arnhem Land decades before.

The moon rose above the tree line, a huge smoke-clouded reddish orb, its light bright enough to read a newspaper by. It lit up the camps where cooking fires burned brightly. Closer to the shore, larger bonfires burned fiercely. People were coming together at the bora ground, their bellies full from feasting on buffalo, wallaby meat, and catfish from the billabong. The hunters had shot scores of geese, ducks, and cockatoos. The feathers littered the ground.

The sacred gathering place, the bora ground, had been used by the people since man first walked the land. The clans gathered there to settle scores and exchange goods, even women, but most of all to dance and sing. Sacred rocks, painstakingly carried from the hills by dreamtime beings, were strategically placed about the billabong flat. For part of the year they were covered by water but once the billabong dried under the merciless dry season sun and exposed the rocks, it signified the timed event of the crocodile corroboree.

The crowd had gathered in numbers, men, women and children. They were all there, several hundred strong, happy and contented, their bellies bloated with good food. Now it was the turn of the dancers and the song men. A dingo howled far off as the full moon lit up the bush. It was like a signal that was instantly answered by the mournful dirge of a didgeridoo before it burst into full melody, accompanied by the strident clapping of ironwood kylie sticks.

Suddenly, some of the dry pandanus leaves fringing the billabong burst into flames, setting the sky on fire and casting ghostly shadows into the water, where the red eyes of crocodiles reflected brightly. It was a cue for the dancers: first the children, many naked, others in shorts, all covered in feathers; they jumped out, their feet stamping the dirt to dust. The dancers almost vanished into the dust cloud, visible only as ghostly, gyrating figures. There were cries of approval, clapping, and loud cheers from proud parents as the kids ended their dance.

Women dressed in colourful waterfowl feathers were next, dancing to a much slower rhythm that told a tale of food gathering in the bush, catching and killing a file snake, or pushing a sharp stick into the face of a crocodile as they waded for lilies and mussel shell fish. Again, there was a roar of approval when the dance ended. The music fell silent.

There was a murmur from the crowd during the lull of the main event. More pandanus leaves flared up and lit the scene as the didgeridoo started off with a slow moaning sound; it droned across the woods and was carried far away to the sea and to the stone country where it echoed off the cliffs. It spoke of sadness, thunder, lightning, and rain; the dry season, when the black cockatoos returned with their baby-like cries; skeins of magpie geese sounding like braying dogs on the wetlands; ducks prattling and dingoes howling. It ended with the harsh cough of the crocodile.

A giant feathered man leapt from the flaming pandanus like a great shadow, naked apart from a pubic tassel worn attached to a skin belt, his head covered with a tall hat made from cockatoo and goose feathers. He stalked across the ground, his shuffling feet throwing up clouds of dust ahead of him. He probed the air with a spear, jamming it into the illusionary prey of the didgeridoo sounds and cries. There was a great roar from the crowd.

'Kangii, Kangii, Kangii!' they shouted again and again as they recognised him.

Ken, lost in the moment, shouted along with them, his heart hammering with the exhilaration of the corroboree. As the music speed increased, so did the stamping of the dancers' feet as they kept pace. Dust rose as the dancer was lost into the shadows and vanished. The crowd roared and applauded with approval.

Now it was the turn of the warriors, armed with jabbing spears; they looked fierce and dangerous, bodies painted with clay and covered with feathers. Dust obscured them as the didgeridoo bellowed and roared, the clack sticks clicking loudly in tune with the war dance. The song man chanted loudly to the drone of the instrument. The crowd clapped their hands and their thighs as the leaping feather-clad performers stamped the ground with their feet, dancing to the savage bursts of song and rhythm. Time stood still …

The moon was high in the sky when Ken walked back to the camp, tired after the long day. For the first time he became aware of lightning that flickered through the trees and the distant moaning of thunder. A storm was coming. A police aide was fast asleep in his swag near the kitchen trailer, snoring loudly. Ken hung his mosquito net from the rope that held up the fly, hoping that the coming rain would not reach in far enough to wet him. Ken noted that the man never stirred as he lay down. He placed his torch and revolver beside his head before pulling the mosquito net over him. He dropped off into a sound sleep.

Ken woke with a start: something had alerted him, something that was part of the shadows in the bush. The aide's snore had changed to a different tone as he rolled over on his other side. But something else was wrong; Ken could sense it, the hair on the nape of his neck was standing up. The didgeridoo and the clap sticks, accompanied by shrill cries and shouts from the billabong, indicated that the festivities were still in full swing on the flat.

Ken gripped his revolver, its weight making him feel secure. An elder had once told him when he was a young boy to never watch a shadow too long, or the imagination would take over. 'That shadow, you look at him, he come alive, and walk up. You look a little, look away and look again, and that shadow, him only shadow.'

Ken remembered those wise words well and looked away, closed his eyes and looked back. Nothing had moved, all appeared as it was before. But Ken also remembered the warning from Kangii. 'Ungara is an owl man, he can see at night.'

Ken had not moved, apart from grabbing his revolver. He relaxed a little, laughing at his fears about moving shadows. He closed his eyes – but was fully alert a second later as the shadows came alive, rushing at him. Ken tried to sit up as something smashed down with force, bursting through the frail net and breaking his left forearm.

Ken fired his revolver, the concussion ringing in his ears, the power flash blinding him. He fired again. There was a shrill cry of pain. Someone ran away, howling like a dingo, and vanished into the shadows. The aide was up, shining a powerful torch and calling out loudly in fear. Ken crept out from under the net, the revolver in his right hand, his left arm hanging helpless by his side.

Suddenly the camp was filled with people. Someone held Ken up; another took the revolver from him. The generator roared into life; lights were switched on. Ken moaned in agony as he was led to a chair and sat down. Questions flew thick and fast. Ken explained what had happened and that the shadows had come alive.

There was a polite cough in the darkness. It was Kangii, holding his spears, looking none the worse after his performances, apart from the feathers still sticking to his body. Jimmy spoke to him and explained what had happened. Kangii grabbed the torch from the aide who was still in shock. He flashed the light about the ground near the mosquito net and grunted in surprise. He stooped down and pointed to where part of an ear lay in the dust. Jimmy picked it up and laughed.

'You got him alright, shot his ear off!' Jimmy exclaimed. 'But maybe you hit him with that other shot too. There is plenty blood and bone splattered on the ground.'

Kangii moved ahead, Jimmy and Hatfield close on his heels. Kangii pointed to a short, thick club and said something. Jimmy spoke for him. 'That the stick that Ungara kills people with. He hurt, never would leave that stick behind. That sacred totem for him.'

Some fifty metres farther on, the men found three short throwing spears and a woomera leaning against a tree. The blood trail led south, towards the stone country. Kangii led the way, the torch guiding the hunting party. No one noted that the moon had vanished or paid any mind to the storm that was heading towards them. It started with a few drops and a flash of lighting that lit up the bush followed by a thunderous clap. With that tremendous sound, the heavens opened, and the storm swept over them.

'It's no use going on,' Hatfield lamented, 'we need to go back and wait for daylight.'

Ken was lying on the ambulance stretcher, his left arm in a sling and attended to by a concerned Adrian Wilson.

'You have to go to Darwin to get that arm fixed, brother,' Adrian said. 'No more hunting Ungara for you. With a bit of luck, he might be dead by now. I hope so. No one is safe with him running around.'

Graham Jenkins landed in a cloud of dust just after daylight. Ken, with his arm in a sling and fortified by pain killers, was helped on board by Wilson and Fields, who was also flying out. As the chopper lifted into the air, they saw that some people were heading for home in their four-wheel-drive vehicles, while others were still in the process of breaking up their camps.

Kangii and Jimmy, along with a young bushwise constable, were in the bush at daylight. They walked for three days, but Ungara had vanished. There were no tracks, no kite hawks or crows feeding on a dead body – nothing. Each day, roaming storms forced them to seek shelter; the wet was near. They turned back to Binjii Billabong to find it deserted, apart from a policeman and two aides who had been ordered to wait for them.

Kangii announced that he was going home for the wet season and started to walk away, but Jimmy called him back and told him that Hatfield had said that they would fly him home in a helicopter from Maningrida in consideration for his services to the police.

Kangii paused; he feared the flying machines, he had never been in a plane of any kind.

'Surely, the man who swims with crocodiles and fears nothing is not afraid to fly in the sky,' Jimmy chided him, reading Kangii's body language.

'No, it will be another step in my life,' Kangii replied bravely as he climbed into the rear of the Toyota Troop Carrier. 'It will be faster. I miss my family.'

9
UNGARA

The moon was high, almost directly overhead, when Ungara stalked the police camp, slipping from shadow to shadow. Someone was moving about under the fly. Ungara saw that it was a police aide. He waited for a long time, listening to the steady drone of the didgeridoo, the clacking of the sticks, and the roar of the dancers and applause of the crowd. Ungara was a patient man. He sat down in the dark shadow, barely metres from the camp. The police aide rolled out his swag and lay down. Ungara decided to kill him with his club, a short heavy instrument about sixty centimetres long. He hefted the curved, beeswax-covered handle and stroked the thick heavy head. The club had been hardened over a fire to almost iron strength.

Ungara had carved it from an ironwood tree buttress root and decorated it with deep, parallel grooves that curved about the head to where it ended in a blunt point. The handle had yellow, red, and white ochre bands circled about it. Ungara placed his spears and the throwing stick against a tree and crept closer, holding the club tightly. Every movement was precise and planned. He felt the ground first with his toes, before placing his feet down, carefully avoiding sticks and leaves that would alert his prey.

Near the fly he brushed into a line that Ken had erected to hang his bush clothes on to dry after washing them. On impulse, Ungara pulled the shirt down and put it on. He knew that camouflage, used in the right conditions, would make him almost invisible. He stalked closer and paused, listening to the snoring of the man he had decided to kill. Suddenly he saw that someone was walking from the corroboree ground towards the camp. Ungara slowly withdrew before stopping in the dense shadows a short distance away.

He watched as Ken put his mosquito net up before climbing under it to sleep. Ungara was pleased when he recognised the hated Balander policeman who was hunting him. He decided to kill both men. He waited before moving again, slowly and without any sudden moves. The shadows were his; he was a shadow. His heart was thumping against his ribs, the adrenalin making him highly alert. He gripped his club tightly and rushed at his prey bringing the heavy club down with deadly force.

Suddenly he was blinded by an intense flaring light; his ear drums almost burst at the noise of the powerful explosion as Ken fired his revolver.

Ungara felt a stunning blow on his face before something hit him like a spear in his waist. The pain was intense. He fell back onto the ground, but with a huge effort he was back on his feet and ran into the night, howling with pain.

He ran a long way before the rain engulfed him. It washed the blood from his face. Ungara stopped, holding his lower rib area where blood was pulsating from a small hole through his fingers. He felt around his back and discovered a gaping hole. Ungara pulled some bark from a paperbark tree, placed it on the body wound, pulled the stolen shirt off and tied it tightly about his waist to hold the bark in place. He cried when he pulled it tight. There was nothing he could do about his face. He touched his cheek bone and felt splintered bone and that his ear was missing. The cold rain washed into the open wounds. Ungara moaned and cried at the intense pain. His ears were still ringing.

Ungara was lucky: the first shot had grazed his left cheek bone, the bullet cutting part of his ear away. But the second shot was the most damaging. The bullet had broken his lower right rib before exiting from his back between his third and fourth rib, missing his spine by millimeters. The pain alone would have killed or crippled a lesser man, but Ungara, born to the bush, was as tough as ironwood. He walked a long way that night, his tracks washed out behind him by the flooding rains.

Ungara knew exactly where he was going – to his own country, where he had been born in a large rock shelter under the lee of a large escarpment outlier. He reached it as the sun rose and lit up the rain-soaked bush. Water lay in shallow depressions while tree leaves and bushes were dripping wet. Even the cracks in the dry earth had closed. But Ungara saw none of it as he crept into the cool open cavern and collapsed onto a large flat rock. He had come home to die.

It was his mother, Lily, who found him, more dead than alive. Ungara did not know that she and his sister, Mary, lived nearby in another shelter.

He had not seen them for many years, nor had he cared for them as a son and brother should. Lily and her daughter had fled from Maningrida after suffering abuse when Ungara first started his killing spree. They had walked for many days before they reached their own country. Lily only had memories of being born there and little else, but her spirits guided her there.

Lily was a tiny, gnome-like woman, who it was rumoured was born after her mother had been raped in her sleep by a stickman, a member of the Mimi-Mimi stone people who live in rock cracks in the stone country. They are shy and very timid. No one had ever seen one, but everyone knew someone who had. Lily was born premature and was white, a rare albino, with pale blue eyes.

Her mother died when Lily uttered her first cry. Someone took her to a mission on the Cadell

River. The missionary and his childless wife had raised the tiny little baby as their own, christening her Lily White. She not only spoke English but also the local language. Lily was partly deformed and almost lame in her left leg; no one liked her, as in their eyes she was extremely ugly and shunned by others in the missionary school.

Later, when she grew up, it was rumoured that Lily was a powerful medicine woman who could point the bone and curse anyone who displeased her to their death.

One day she ran away into the bush. A small tribal clan took her in and tolerated her, though they were not kind. One night she crept into a shelter where a man was sleeping. He took her and made love to her all night, delighted that his dreams had come true. But it was said that when he woke up in the morning and saw Lily beside him, he felt so shameful that he ran to a big waterhole where he sat on a sandy strip near deep water chanting mournful songs for forgiveness of what he had done. When night fell a crocodile took him away.

Ungara was born from that union, and, like his mother, he was a small baby and very ugly. He had inherited her pale blue eyes, which were in sharp contrast to his black skin. But his mother loved him and ensured that he was never hungry. When Ungara turned twelve years old, he, along with others of his own age, was taken into the bush for the man-making ceremony. But Ungara was not circumcised, because he ran away into the bush to avoid the pain. Later, when he returned, everyone laughed at him and called him names and a coward. He hated them all with a passion and fled into the night. His mother found him and comforted him. After that they lived alone in the bush.

A year later, while spearing fish in a billabong, Ungara heard his mother scream in terror. He ran as fast as he could to where the screams had come from. They led him to where his mother was being raped by a big naked man.

Ungara did not hesitate and drove his spear deep into the man's back. He cried in pain and rolled off Lily and onto his back, breaking the spear and driving it deeper into his body until the point protruded from his chest. Ungara picked up a big rock and smashed it into the man's head. It was his first kill. It gave him a feeling of immense power.

Lily gave birth to Mary nine months later. There was no one to help her. Unlike her brother, Mary was a normal sized baby, but too big for tiny Lily; she could not open wide enough, causing damage to the baby's head, leaving her slow and dim as she grew up. Two wet seasons later Ungara left his homeland, leaving Lily and Mary to fend for themselves in the cave complex. He travelled for many days to the north, discovering places that he did not know existed.

One day he was walking along a track when a Toyota trayback drove by in a cloud of dust. There were several people in the back. They saw Ungara hiding behind a pandanus palm and yelled to the driver to stop. The vehicle reversed and though he was frightened, the boy took up the invite to go with the hunting party to their homeland.

Ungara was adopted by an old man, an artist who painted on bark and made weapons – spears, axes, clubs and other implements that he bartered for food or sold to the Maningrida Art Gallery. He was too old to hunt, and he cunningly gave the boy a place in the clan so that he could provide for him, which the young hunter did very well. In return the old man taught him his art and treated him like a son.

Ungara loved his new home and was well liked, as he excelled in hunting and fishing. No one could match him in impromptu spear throwing competitions, while his skill with the fighting stick was talked about in the hunting camps. Even though he was a head smaller than anyone of his own age, he was lighting fast and had extraordinary reflexes that enabled him to dodge and weave about an opponent.

But Ungara had no luck at all with the young girls. When they saw his small penis, they would laugh and make fun of him. He hated them. One day Ungara raped a ten-year-old girl.

Everyone was angry and there were cries from the women to castrate and kill him. Ungara fled, the spearmen close at his heels. But they lost his track a day later. He vanished but sometime later the bush telegraph spoke of someone who would sneak into shelters and homes at night and rape young girls. No one ever saw him; even the white police could find no trace or match the fingerprints they took.

One night his luck ran out in a small house when a struggling young girl cried in fear when he touched her. Her father rushed to her aid, armed with a torch and a butcher's knife. Ungara fled through an open window. The father was able to provide a good description of the assailant. There was only one man that fitted it – Ungara. But someone warned him, and from that time on he kept out of communities and villages.

Now he had come home to die. His wounds were festering; he lost consciousness and remained in a coma for many days. But Lily attended him with a love that only a mother has. As a medicine woman, much of which she had learned from her Balanda foster mother, she knew how to make poultices and let maggots eat the dead skin. She chewed food and forced Ungara to eat it.

All through that wet season she attended him. He healed slowly and one day he was able to sit up. Lily taught him how to walk again, but it took many days. For long weeks Ungara lived in pain. It affected his mind and instilled into him a great hatred for the police. But it was his insatiable urge for sex that drove him back into the bush; one day, Lily found him having sex with his sibling. Enraged, she attacked him. He hit her hard and she fell back against a rock, splitting her head open. Mary screamed in rage and attacked her brother. Ungara grabbed her by the throat and held her until she stopped struggling. Only then did he flee, leaving his deceased family behind.

10
THE RESURRECTION

Ungara was pleased with his work. He hefted his new fighting club in his hands and took swings at imaginary foes. He had worked long and hard to create the weapon, carving it from an ironwood root with a knife he had taken from his mother's shelter. He had hardened the timber over a fire and painstakingly carved totemic images into the surface, then painted it with ochre he had gathered in the creek.

He had also made four throwing spears and a woomera to send the missile into its target. The spears were made from hardwood shafts and tipped with sharp fire-hardened barbs. They were only about two metres long, unlike the long ceremonial and fish spears twice their length. Ungara excelled with this sort of spear, which was favoured by the warriors of times past for battle because they possessed great accuracy in the hands of an expert marksman.

The wet season was over, the grasses were ripe, and the birds were breeding. The people were moving out of the communities back to the homeland camps and houses, where hungry dogs were waiting for them with wagging tails. They had been left to their own resources when the people moved out for the wet season. Big 'knock-em-down' storms still roamed the land, their strong winds knocking down the ripe grass and old trees that nature no longer had need for. It was Banggerdeng time, the onset of the dry season.

Ungara had found a homeland dwelling and made it his own. It was made from clay brick and he enjoyed the company of many dogs. He felt a strong urge for a woman but knew that it was time to move on before he was discovered. The homeland was a large one with several houses, a school, teacher accommodation, community centre, and power station. When Ungara heard a vehicle approaching, he fled, taking his meager belongings with him. He hid in the long grass, invisible to the naked eye.

The vehicle, a Toyota trayback, was driven by a Balander man. A slim-bodied Balander woman with blonde hair was with him. The vehicle pulled up near the schoolhouse. Ungara watched them as they cleaned the house and carried their belongings in. The man walked to the power station, carrying a drum of fuel. The generator kicked into life a few minutes later.

Ungara's heart missed a beat when he saw the woman come out of the house, completely naked. He had never seen a Balander woman naked before and he thought she looked very beautiful. His sexual urge increased when the man embraced the woman and stroked her breasts before feeling between her legs. He then carried her inside the house.

Ungara, his passion fully aroused, stalked to the house, his movement slow and precise. He peered through the window and saw the couple on the bed. They were making love, letting out lots of pleasant sounds.

Ungara walked to the door and slowly opened it. It gave a small creak, and then he shoved it open and rushed at the couple. The woman screamed in terror as Ungara's fighting club slammed down on the man's skull, caving it in.

Ungara hit her next, a soft blow that only dazed her. He pulled the man off the bed and mounted the sobbing protesting woman. He grabbed her by her throat and tightened his grip until he was finished. She did not move. Ungara became aware of the dogs barking and the noise of approaching vehicles. He grabbed his belongings and fled into the thick bush. No one saw him.

Sergeant Ken Wilson was back on duty after long sickness leave to heal his broken limb. He and Linda had fallen in love and married. He watched her as she walked towards the police station from the police house, her belly showing a small bump of advanced pregnancy. He heard her talking to the duty officer before she stepped into his office. They embraced and held each other. Ken held her away and looked into her eyes.

'Did you sleep well? I didn't have the heart to wake you this morning,' he said.

'I did, darling, but baby woke me up. It kicked me – there! It's doing it again.'

She placed Ken's hand on her belly. He felt the tiny movement and the magic of the moment.

'Wow, that's amazing. That's the first time I've ever felt that,' Ken said as he hugged and kissed her.

His phone rang. It annoyed Ken, but his was a secure number known to only senior police officers. He reluctantly released Linda and picked the handpiece up.

'Sergeant Ken Wilson, Balanya police.'

'Ken – Peter here,' came the grim voice over the phone. 'Bad news, I'm afraid. A schoolteacher on the upper Liverpool River homeland has been clubbed to death and his wife raped. She's lucky to be alive. All the hallmarks point to one man – Ungara. It looks like he's back from the dead. Hatfield is in charge of the investigation as it's in his area. But I need you in the field to hunt Ungara down once and for all. You're the best man for the job and know his habits. Graham Jenkins will be available to you and will drop you off on the Liverpool. Take anyone you want and let me know if you need anything. Senior Constable Raines will fill in for you during your absence.'

'Fuck. That's the last thing I wanted to hear, Peter. I still have nightmares just thinking about that bastard. I'll take Toby with me. He also has a score to settle with Ungara. What about Jimmy Cooper, any chance having him seconded to me?'

'Done, Ken, I'm sure Hatfield will cooperate with you. What about Kangii?'

'Kangii will find us if he wants to help, I am sure of that. I'll be in touch, same phone, same time as usual. Bye for now.'

Ken hung up and looked at Linda. 'I'm sorry darling, but I need to go on patrol. Ungara is still alive. He killed a schoolteacher and raped his wife. It's my job.'

'Of course, my love. I knew that when I married you. Just be careful out there, I want you to come back to me soon,' Linda cried, wiping tears from her eyes.

Ken called Toby on the radio and asked him to come to the office. 'I won't be long, Ken. I am just sorting out a little family disagreement between a husband and wife,' Toby replied. Ken readied his gear, again traveling light and being prepared to live from the land, unlike other officers who took big packs loaded with food and other supplies. Ken's upbringing on the floodplains and his bush adventures with his Indigenous playmates had prepared him well for the task.

Toby sat down in shock when Ken told him the bad news. 'Fuck, Ken, that is not what I need. I'd talked myself into believing that you killed him, but you must have only wounded him. If he's healed from that, then take my word for it: he'll be more dangerous than ever. He's overstepped the mark now seeing he is killing Balanders and raping their women. He no longer cares.'

The men were in the air an hour later, enthralled by brimming billabongs, flowing rivers, creeks, and swamps that spread to far horizons amongst the woodland.

'We had a great wet season, Ken,' Jenkins said. 'Watch yourself – the country's full of snakes and crocodiles. I wouldn't be walking down there in that long grass for a million dollars.'

Hatfield greeted them somberly when the helicopter touched down in an open space between the buildings. Only two police vehicles were present. Everyone else had fled back to Maningrida.

'G'day Ken, hello Toby, it's good to see you both,' he said, shaking their hands. 'Though I wish we could be meeting again in happier circumstances. The killing and the rape happened earlier this morning and was reported to me about an hour after it happened by a phone call. There's a phone in that building and good reception from the tower. Most of them are hit by lighting during the wet season, but this one escaped. We passed several vehicles on the way in, fleeing back to Maningrida. One had the woman. We put her in an ambulance that was following us. Forensics flew out in a chartered helicopter not long ago. They took the body with them.'

Hatfield filled them in on the other details. He was more than happy to let Jimmy Cooper go with them if he wanted to.

'Jimmy and Constable Dave Reed are somewhere out there looking for tracks. Ungara must have lived here in the Wet. He made new weapons, so he'll be well armed. The schoolteachers were with the home coming convoy, but when the people pulled up to fish a billabong, they continued. It appears that they took the advantage of being alone and made love, not knowing that Ungara was watching.

Hell of a thing to happen to anyone. That poor woman will never forget this - if she lives. She's lucky to be alive. Hello, the boys are back.'

Ken and Toby shook hands with Jimmy and Dave Reed, a young but bush-wise constable who was on his first bush transfer from Darwin.

'That track bin gone in that stone country, that way,' Jimmy said in Kriol. 'We look hard, but nothing. One thing sure, though, that track belong to Ungara. I bin know that.'

'Jimmy, Ken and Toby will be hunting him down. Ken would like you to go along. You want to go?' Hatfield asked.

'Mah, hell yeah, boss,' Jimmy replied with enthusiasm. 'Mah, I reckon we'll catch him alright. We go now.'

'Yes, mate,' Ken answered. 'Grab your gear and let's get going.'

The trackers found the killer's track some distance from where Jimmy had lost it. Ungara's tracks headed east, which appeared out of character as they expected him to seek the sanctuary of the stone country. He had made little effort in hiding them, which confused the trackers. All afternoon they kept on. It wasn't until the sun began to fade and sink below the horizon in a blood red orb that the hunters pulled up and made camp beside a large creek pool.

11

THE KILLINGS

After having enjoyed the customary mug of sweet black tea at daylight the men were back on the tracks. Ken was studying his topographic map when Jimmy came up and pointed to a dot on it.

'I reckon that Ungara may go there, to Arufura Camp,' he said in his heavily accented Kriol. 'I reckon he might raid that place little bit long way from here. Two places, one for young boys, this one for young girls. Those kids play up in community and the elders send them to these places to learn proper culture and respect.'

Ken knew about the bush centres, as he had sent several kids who had run afoul of the law there from his own community. Both centres were Aboriginal projects that were set up with Government grants in order to curb crime in communities. The police had no control of the centres, and they were regarded as 'blackfella business'.

The bush telegraph had it that volunteer elders ruled the camps with an iron hand and that they were highly successful. Ken knew of several young people who had become role models when they returned after spending a dry season learning proper social skills.

'Maybe grab young girl at this place and kill others,' Jimmy said, alarm in his voice.

'Do they have a phone there?' Ken asked.

'Nothing, no car, only boat for fishing,' Jimmy replied. 'Maybe you call that Ramingining police mob, they bin closer with Toyota.'

Ken called Inspector Fields and informed him of Jimmy's fears. 'I'll get onto it, Ken. What is your current position? I'll get Jenkins to pick you up. By the looks of it you still have the better part of a day's travel ahead of you.'

'More than that, Peter. It's just too hot and humid to travel in the middle of the day. It would be good if we had another hunting party in the field and the full use of a helicopter. We could use it for an aerial search and to pick one party up and put it in the expected path of Ungara.'

'I've been working on that, Ken. The politicians have been slow with funding, but there's been a huge outcry from the public and I expect that by the end of the day I'll have a gold credit card to use as I see fit. Okay, Ken, leave it with me. Cheers.'

Ken informed the trackers of what the boss told them. 'Let's find a shady place and wait at that creek over there. Let's go.'

Jimmy speared a large saratoga, a primitive slab-sided bony fish. He cooked it over the coals of a small fire that Ken had lit while the trackers were hunting. When it was done, the men picked at the flesh with their fingers, carefully avoiding the small bones. It was tasty and welcome.

'How come white fella like you live in the bush all the same as blackfella, Ken?' Jimmy asked. 'All that other Balander policeman take too much supermarket tucker and all that rubbish.'

Ken knew it was a huge compliment, a rare one from an Indigenous man.

'I was born on the Wild Man River plains and lived there until I went to school, Jimmy. My play mates were people like you and Toby. We hunted and fished and went to school all the same one mob. My mother was the schoolteacher. There were no black fellers or Balanders in her class, only people. Everyone was the same.'

'That tells a lot,' Jimmy mused. 'What about you Toby? You don't talk that Kriol, but proper English like Ken.'

'I went to Balander school in Darwin and university, Jimmy. But that country of mine called to me all the time, so I went back and became a policeman instead of a lawyer in the big smoke.'

The sound of a helicopter coming from the west had the men running for open ground. The chopper went over them, did a tight turn and came in low over the trees before touching down in a cloud of dust and grass seeds. The men stepped on board and were in the air in minutes.

Ahead lay the Arafura Swamp, one of the largest freshwater swamps in Australia: over 500 square kilometres of streams, marsh, and paperbark groves growing on high spots that only appear in the dry season. It spread before them, the east border lost in a shimmering mirage.

'Bloody hell,' Ken swore. 'If Ungara heads into it we'll never find him.'

A police vehicle was parked near a building. Jenkins dropped the R44 in a tight clearing and landed in a swirling cloud of dust. Ken waited until the dust cleared before opening the door and stepping out, followed by his men.

A solid, short-statured man with a florid face and a large overflowing stomach shook hands with Ken.

'Good to see you, Ken. We got here as fast as we could, but nothing appears to be out of order. We don't come here too often unless we drop someone off that we reckon needs a second chance in life instead of prison. Odd, though – there's no one about. They may be out fishing or hunting; the boys are checking by the river. We only arrived a few minutes ago.'

Ken had met Sergeant Steve Marriott before. Despite his appearance, he had a reputation of being a fair and excellent officer who knew and understood the ways of the tribal people in Arnhem Land. However, Marriott was an alcoholic and only suited for remote bush stations where alcohol was not permitted. He was unable to function in large towns due to his constant need for booze.

A loud cry of alarm sounded from the direction of the Goyder River. Everyone rushed down the narrow path that led under tall shady paperbarks to a large pandanus and Geebung palm-lined pool. Three men, a white constable and two police aides, were standing around two bodies lying on the riverbank. Behind them, two dinghies partly filled with water, floated in the river.

'Fuck, Sergeant,' constable Wayne Dickson cried in anguish, 'it's old Buna and Nippa! The poor old bastards have been bludgeoned to death. They never stood a chance.'

Ken recognised the signature of Ungara and his killer club. 'Ungara's work. The bastard is mad,' he swore. 'He's killing anyone that he comes in contact with.'

Someone called out from the cover of the thick scrub nearby, a small choked cry of help. They rushed over to find a young boy of about fourteen years of age lying under a scrubby bush. The trackers slowly lifted him out. His head was soaked in dried blood and his right arm was hanging motionless by his side. He spoke incoherently, his words slurred and in pain. One of Marriot's trackers spoke for him in Kriol.

'Ungara come. Him and some other boys kill everyone. This boy hit hard with club, but bin run away in the bush. He say that nuther one in bush alonga river, maybe hurt bad. He say it was Ungara because he has blue eyes all the same like

Balander. He say that Ungara mob sink the tinnies and take 'nuther one up river.'

'Okay, boys, spread out and find the others,' Marriot ordered harshly. 'You – police boy fella, you look after this boy properly. Take him to the hut. That bloody Ungara is setting up his own mob. That's what he came here for. I'll bet he's raiding the girls' camp right now.'

'That's what I was thinking,' Ken said. 'Toby, you come with me. You too, Jack. We'll use the helicopter. Let's move.'

They were soon up in the air and landed minutes later between two galvanized iron sheds. Ken was out first, his .357 Magnum S&W revolver in his hands. Marriott and Toby were alongside him, their service Glocks ready. Ken pointed and indicated to Marriott to check the other shed. Toby was close on Ken's heels as he pushed the door open and swore loudly.

'Fuck, this isn't right,' Ken swore as he saw the bodies of an elderly couple and a young girl on the blood-soaked floor, their heads bashed in. 'Ungara's work. The bastard beat us by an hour at least.'

Marriot yelled out from the other shed, a strange tone in his voice. 'Over here, Ken. Two dead girls – both raped and bashed to death, by the looks of it. The bastard is fucking mad. He needs to be shot on sight like a mad dog.'

Toby had walked into the bush, his eyes glued on the ground in front of him. Suddenly someone broke cover from the low scrub and ran into the open bush.

Toby ran as fast as he could, his breath coming in gasps, before he caught up and tackled the fugitive almost 300 metres from where the chase had started. Toby saw that it was a young girl. She screamed in terror, her hands clawing at his face. Toby grabbed her by her wrists and held her, yelling at her to stop and that he would not hurt her. She stopped and started sobbing.

Toby let her go and sat alongside her holding her shoulders. Only when she had stopped crying did he lift her tiny body up into his arms, carrying her to the buildings. Marriott recognised her instantly. She and two other girls had been sent to the camp after being involved in stealing fuel from planes to sniff and get high.

'Shirley, what happened here? Where are the other girls?' Marriott asked gently.

'They bin gone bush with that Ungara and that Chicken George, along with that mob that kill others,' she replied, tears in her eyes. 'Me run away in bush and hide. That mob bin gone in that boat and in that swamp.'

'Who is Chicken George?' Marriott asked.

'Him bin bad Darwin boy, he was in boys' camp, but they bully and rape him, so he come to girl camp.'

'I know him,' Ken said. 'He's a long-grasser from Darwin who lived in Balanya for a season with some relatives. He and two others broke into the store and were caught. He's a real piece of shit and should have been sent to jail, but the elders interjected and asked the court to have the culprits handed over for tribal punishment. The Justice of the Peace agreed and that was the last I saw of them. I wonder why Ungara didn't kill him?'

Ken informed Inspector Fields of the gruesome killings. Fields ordered him to continue to search the swamp in the helicopter and said that a field team would be sent immediately by helicopter to take care of the bodies.

'Steve can take charge of the centres and report directly to me. You and Toby take to the air and search the swamp as much as you can. If you spot Ungara, you know what to do. Base yourself at Ramingining until further notice. That includes Jenkins and his chopper. Use it for the search.'

12

SANCTUARY

A thousand channels separated by a million islands; a drowned land, the domain of dinosaurs, Ken thought as Jenkins flew the R44 above the endless mosaic of trees, billabongs, and streams. Flocks of snow-white egrets and corellas painted the swamp like a miniature snowstorm as they rose with panic-stricken wings below the helicopter. Skeins of magpie geese and ducks panicked when the swishing blades neared them. Buffalo stampeded and massive crocodiles slipped from banks into the lily-clad water. Soon the swamp was alive with myriad alarmed and airborne waterfowl that in sections almost blackened the sky, but there were no signs of the fugitives.

There was nothing; they had vanished into a primeval void. 'I have to head back,' Jenkins announced. 'I need more fuel. This is one place I don't want to land in if we run out of it. Bloody hell, look at the size of that bastard, he must be eight metres long.'

Jenkins pointed to where a crocodile of gigantic size was basking on a grassy bank. 'With a bit of luck, Ungara might be eaten by something like that. There's no way in hell I'd even consider fleeing in there.'

'But he has, and I don't think we'll be finding him anytime soon. There's more chance of finding the proverbial needle in the haystack,' Ken replied. 'Let's head to Ramingining. I'm looking forward to a hot shower and a meal.'

They were in the air at daybreak, looking for the tell-tale of campfire smoke, but nothing could be seen apart from the never-ending spectacle of waterfowl masses. There were others on the swamp; Marriott and two trackers were on the water in a police boat, along with a hired council boat manned by Constable Dickson and two police aides, Billy and Butcha. Together with the eyes in the sky, the three parties worked as a team.

The next day, three other boats manned by police and trackers joined the search. They were out of Darwin and had been landed by barge overnight at Nangalala. Another helicopter and a fixed wing plane reinforced the search teams. The hunt continued for two weeks, but the swamp revealed nothing.

The ABC and the Darwin media came and went. As usual in line with urban journalists' thinking, they were highly critical of the police methods and there were demands for the police commissioner and Inspector Fields to resign. When that was ignored, they screamed for the blood of the Police Minister. In the meantime, the police parties involved in the search were pushed to extremes in the swamp. Mosquito hordes attacked them without let up, while snakes and crocodiles made any mistake a fatal one.

A tracker was attacked by a crocodile when he waded ashore in shallow water. A hail of bullets saved him from serious injury, but the attack indicated just how dangerous the swamp truly was.

Fields called a meeting at Ramingining. It was attended by the Police Commissioner, Darrel Simmons and senior police involved in the search. There was a lot of talk and much soul searching. It ended with the hunt being called off on the insistence of Ken Wilson.

'Look, we don't even know if Ungara and his mob are in the swamp, or if they were ever in it at all. As far as we know they might be in the Stone Country laughing at us. We could do this forever and still get no results. It's impossible to find signs in there; there are no tracks, no signs of campfire or shelters, nothing, only bloody big monster crocodiles. The best we can do is withdraw and wait until he makes his next move.'

The dry season was ending when Linda gave birth to a healthy baby boy in the Darwin Base Hospital. Ken had hired an apartment and taken leave. They lived in the city for three weeks before heading home to Arnhem Land. The dry season was well advanced, the land drying and withering up under the relentless sun. The East Alligator River had stopped flowing and Red Lily Billabong was almost dry.

Ken and Linda settled into married life with a baby, though the police station was busy as usual; perhaps even more so, thanks to the drought-like conditions, better known as the troppo or mango season, putting everyone on edge. For some it meant that tempers ran hot. Grog running, always a problem, increased tenfold in the troppo season. It kept the police busy.

Ken looked out across the sunbaked plain that lay shimmering under the mirage. The office air conditioner was working overtime and he silently thanked whoever had invented it, because life without it would be almost unbearable. The phone rang.

'Ken, Peter here,' came the familiar voice. 'Bad news, I'm afraid. Ungara and his mob are on the move. They attacked a buffalo safari hunting party on Annie Creek. One man was speared but he'll make it. The operator, Kurt Moray, opened fire on the attackers with a handgun and killed a young boy. The others fled. Wayne Dickson is on his way to investigate the attack. I need you and Toby to go there and take up the tracks. Jenkins should be there shortly to pick you up.'

Ken radioed Toby, who was on patrol at Cahill's Crossing, and told him to return ASAP. He packed the gear they needed and informed Senior Constable Sue Raines that she was in charge until he returned. Ken headed home and told Linda the bad news. She clung to him for a long time before letting him go.

'Please be careful, darling. Little Ken and I need you.'

Toby was waiting at the police station. 'I expected this, Ken. Ungara will be heading to the Stone Country before the wet season flushes him out of the swamp. At least now we have a chance of tracking him and his mob.'

The phone rang as the men walked out. Sue called out to Ken to say it was Inspector Fields and that it was urgent.

'Ken… terrible news, I'm afraid,' said Fields, grief evident in his voice. 'Wayne Dickson, Billie, and Butcha are dead. I just got word from Steve. It seems they were ambushed and speared at the Annie Creek crossing. Their vehicle was set alight. It was reported by sat phone from council workers who were inspecting the Central Arnhem Road. Steve is on his way, but it'll take him time to get there. By the way – you'd better take your rifles, the police arms are missing. Ungara's mob is now armed with modern weapons. Ken, get over there. You know what to do. I'll have reinforcements join you in the morning. Wait for them. That's an order.'

It appeared to take hours before Jenkins descended the R44 down from the heights of the Stone Country to the monsoon forests below, where a vehicle was parked near the burned-out hulk of the police Toyota Troop Carrier. They landed in a choking plume of dust and ashes left from the fire that had set the surrounding bush alight. It was still smoldering.

'G'day Ken,' Marriott greeted Ken before shaking hands with the three men. 'What a fucking day. Wayne and my two best aides have been murdered in cold blood. Not sure what happened, but Eddie over there says that they must have come across foot tracks on the road and decided to investigate. Wayne and Billy were speared in that rocky outcrop over there. Butcha fled and almost made it to the vehicle before being speared in the back.'

Marriott, a tough man, was shaking and there was a tremor in his voice. 'The murdering bastards stole their weapons, one Glock pistol and three scope-sighted .308 Remington rifles. There would have been about 100 rounds of ammunition in the Toyota also,' he said, alarm in his voice. 'Ken, this is a whole new ball game. Ungara now has his own mob and they're not afraid to kill anyone they come across. We need to stop him in his tracks before more young idiots take it into their heads to join the outlaws.'

The sound of a large helicopter came from the west. A few minutes later an Army Blackhawk helicopter landed some distance away, its huge rotors setting up a cloud of spiraling dust. Several people disembarked when it cleared. Ken recognized Inspector Peter Fields, the Police Commissioner Darrel Simmons, and the forensic team, Doctor

Joe Hockey and Abbie Perkins. There was also another person that Fields introduced as Chaplain John Sterling, the police chaplain and counselor. The two army pilots remained at the Blackhawk.

The men shook hands, the meeting sombre and painful. The Northern Territory Police Force is only a small one and most officers know one another. The forensic team went about their grisly task as the police officers sat under a shady tree and discussed the event and the actions to be taken. Sterling, Marriott, and his aides, Job and Nono, were sitting under a shady tree some distance away.

Fields took Ken aside and asked him how Marriott was handling the situation.

'Not real good, Peter, or Job and Nono either. They were best mates with the deceased and were very close to them.'

'I thought so, Ken. I'd like to get Steve away somewhere else, but we both know that if he got near a pub he'd wipe himself out on the piss. No, I have a good man with me to help him get over this. No one is better qualified for the job than Pastor John; he'll stay and help him and the others to heal. Best I leave Steve where he is and keep him away from grog. Okay, let's see what the boss has to say.'

Simmons, a Territory born career police officer, knew what his men were facing in the trackless wilderness of Arnhem Land. He had served in remote communities twenty years ago and understood what lay ahead better than anyone.

'Ken,' Simmons said. 'I know you are keen to get started while the tracks are still hot, but we now have a situation where you are no longer facing a lone wolf, but several young hot heads that are now well armed. Thanks to our Federal member, the army has offered us air support if we wish to land our men anywhere at a moment's notice. We have a Rapid Response Team on standby and the Blackhawk is totally at our disposal until this whole thing ends, one way or another. It will be stationed at Jabiru. I've discussed the tactics at length with Peter, who is in charge. Over to you, Peter.'

'Okay, blokes, Senior Constable Jack Harney is on the way from Burunga with two police aides, David and Joey. They'll be part of Ken's team. You all know Jack – he has a similar background as Ken, a busman born and bred on Mainoru Station. He roamed the lower stone country with his mother's people until his dad sent him off to school in Katherine. Jack's our best man when it comes to stone country knowhow. I sent a helicopter to pick them up, they should arrive soon. Okay, looks like Joe and Abbie need a hand with the body bags. Their job is done here, but ours is just starting.'

Ken and Steve watched as the Blackhawk vanished into the setting sun, trailing a huge dust plume from where it had taken off. Inspector Field remained behind. Jenkins had departed earlier, as they had no need for his services anymore.

Someone had lit a fire and was preparing dinner when another chopper sounded from the south. It landed where the Blackhawk had taken off from minutes earlier. Fields greeted the new arrivals and introduced them to Ken, Marriott and the police aides. Ken had met Jack Harney before.

Jack was rated as a legend for his exploits in keeping peace and jailing criminals in the Katherine-Roper River region.

Jack was of similar build as Ken, tall and rangy with sinewy muscles that indicated endurance and strength. His nose was set at an angle, the result of college rugby union. He laughed a lot and was known for his never-ending jokes.

'G'day Ken,' Harney greeted Ken as they shook hands, 'great to catch up again. Mate, I am looking forward to working with you. Not too many people could have done what you did to Ungara last year.'

Inspector Fields gave the two men more instructions before boarding the helicopter that had brought Harney and his crew in. 'You have your instructions,' were his last words. 'As usual, contact me on a daily basis, and don't forget to call Linda, Ken – as if I need to tell you.'

The men enjoyed thick steaks cooked on the campfire coals. The supplies and other rations had been dropped in by the Blackhawk.

'Better enjoy them,' said Ken. 'We're on bush tucker when we hit the tracks tomorrow. Bit of a weak moon tonight. I want a guard out all the time at night; everyone can take turns doing it. You all know that Ungara can see in the dark – something I'll never forget when he attacked me last year. In the morning we'll take only the rations and gear we need.

No fancy food and no large packs to haul about. Everyone will be armed with a .308 rifle, 30 rounds of ammunition and pistols for those issued with one. But there will be no shooting unless Jack or I give the order, or if you are attacked. Steve will take any gear that we don't need back with him.'

The men sat around the friendly fire that bonded them together; beyond the circle of light lay evil. Nearby, deeply concealed in thick scrub, Ungara and two of his boys waited for the men to fall asleep so they could attack. Jack took the first shift, highly alert as if sensing the danger in the surrounding shadows.

Ungara whispered to the boys; they followed him and slipped away towards the distant escarpment. Ungara was a patient man. He would kill the hated Balander police another day.

13

TRAPPED

Ken wiped his eyes to make sure that the light wasn't tricking him into seeing things. He had been woken by Toby to take up the watchdog duties an hour before daylight and was in the process of lighting the fire for breakfast when he saw movement in the bush close by.

'Kangii!' Ken exclaimed loudly, a big smile on his face. 'Welcome, old friend.'

Ken's reaction alerted everyone. Jack leaped up and drew his Glock, but Ken pushed his arm down. 'Relax, Jack, it's Kangii, the greatest tracker in Arnhem Land. He's come to help.'

'Kangii? I thought he was a shadow – a myth, a bush legend,' Jack replied in awe, pushing the Glock back in its holster.

Kangii strode into the camp as if he had never left it, his tall raw-boned body glistening with oiled muscles that flexed like steel cords with every movement. Apart from a wallaby skin belt, a woven bag, a small stone knife, and a flap of skin hanging from his hips that covered his genitals, he was naked as usual. He carried three short throwing spears and a throwing stick.

Jack had heard of Kangii and had chased him on two occasions when murderers were speared near Weemoll on the orders of the elders. But the trackers had lost the tracks – or perhaps were unwilling to follow them. To the people of Arnhem Land, Kangii was as mysterious as the land itself, a tribal myth perpetuated by legends that were whispered about the campfires of the old people. Kangii was a legendary figure, an invisible man who sometimes walked the land to swim with crocodiles or executed the law of the elders with deadly force.

Kangii held Ken by the shoulder before repeating the same process with Toby. They had become good friends; they were as close as anyone, apart from his family, would ever get to the Kurdaitchii man.

'He says that it's good to see you, Ken,' Toby interpreted. 'He heard that Ungara had broken out of the swamp and that more people have been killed. The tribal elders have given him total control of Ungara's life. He wants to know who these other people are and why we need so many to hunt one man.'

Tony introduced Jack and Marriott and the trackers. After the pleasantries were over, Ken asked Toby to explain in detail what had happened the day before and their plans of attack.

Kangii grunted in reply when Toby finished and looked about the gathering before speaking. Toby spoke for him, a frown on his forehead.

'He says that Steve and Job are sorry for their friends' deaths. He says they should not come because they have no control over their heads. He says that Nono only wants revenge and should not come along.'

Marriott looked at Kangii, a deep frown above his eyes that showed the strain on his mind. There was no anger in his voice, only respect. 'Tell him, Toby, that he is a very smart man and is totally correct. But also tell him that I and my men have been ordered not to go, but I will let Nono go if he wants to.'

'I will go,' Nono replied slowly and decisively. 'Two of those girls are my brother's children. I want them back for my family.'

'Okay, it's done then,' Ken said. 'We're wasting time, let's pack up and hit the tracks.'

It was Kangii who picked up the tracks of the night's visitors who had spied on the camp forty metres away. Kangii pointed at the footprints and grunted, 'Ungara.'

'Fuck,' exclaimed Jack. 'The mongrels were watching us all the time. You were right about putting a guard out, Ken. They would have killed us in our sleep.'

Ungara and his boys had made no attempt to cover their tracks. With the trackers setting a cracking pace, they saw tantalizing views of the distant escarpment over the trees by midday. It was the extreme humidity and sun that forced them to seek the relative coolness of a deep cave recess in an outlier that rose tall above the woodlands.

Others had been there before them. The shelter had been used for thousands of years by people who had painted murals of their totem animals on the walls. There were hand stencils of children and adults in white clay, the yellow and brown ochre images of wallaroos, fish, crocodiles, and birds, a vault where time had stood still. The men looked about in awe and respect as they viewed a culture that had been lost in the annals of time.

The trackers were busy, walking back and forward, pointing at fresh footprints in the dust and ashes of the shelter floor. They reminded Ken of bloodhounds.

'That Ungara mob bin here, they bin camp this place, but bin go this morning,' Nono reported when he returned. 'Bin many girls and boys. They bin eat rock wallaby in other one cave. Kangii and other trackers still bin look.'

Kangii, as always, took the lead when the men headed out, all feeling a little refreshed from their break, though the heat was still intense. Ahead, an open, termite-studded burned plain shimmered like a living thing in a mirage against the backdrop of a large escarpment outlier. Illusionary buffalo and brolgas stood in shady tree groves on impossible long legs, seemingly five metres tall in the shivering reflections of the heat haze.

'Billabong,' Toby spoke for Kangii. 'He says we should be careful as he reckons it might be a good place for an ambush. He says that the buffalo might not want to give up their water either and may charge us and drive us away.'

'Spread out,' Ken ordered, 'And make sure that your rifles are loaded, safety catch on. Shoot back if we're fired on, or if the buffalo charge.'

The men spread apart, their feet kicking up small dust plumes on the dry, fire-blackened plain. A flock of egrets rose from amongst the trees; a split second later, a shot echoed across the plain, the bullet hitting to the left of Kangii and ricocheting away behind him, leaving a dust plume in its wake. The brolgas rose en-masse on madly flapped panic-stricken wings, protesting with loud trumpeting as the buffalo herd stampeded and vanished towards the outlier.

Jack saw movement under the shadows of a paperbark tree. He fired two rapid shots with his rifle. There was no return fire. The men ran, dodging and weaving as fast as they could. They reached the cover of the trees, gasping for breath. A young boy, clutching a stolen police rifle, lay under the tree crying in pain from a bullet wound in his upper leg. Jack pulled the rifle from his hands and handed his and the other rifle to David before unlimbering his pack. He pulled a small first aide kit from it and took out a pressure bandage. Ken marveled at his skill in dressing the wound. It stopped the bleeding immediately.

'It's a deep wound, Ken. The bullet went right through, but it missed the bone. He will recover if we can get him to a hospital soon. Who you, boy, what your name?'

'Me bin Harry. Me bin from Maningrida,' the boy replied in pain, his eyes tear-flecked. 'That Ungara say me bin shoot everyone. But that big gun, he bin kick me proper hard.'

'Where that Ungara mob bin go?' Ken asked.

'Bin go there in stone country, but only mob. That Ungara and Chicken George bin go to Balanya, kill policemen and Balanders.'

'Fuck,' Ken cursed. 'I need to go home and protect my family. Where is that bloody sat-phone?'

Ken spoke at length to Inspector Fields on what Ungara was intending. 'It will take him four or five days to get there, Peter. But I need an urgent medi-vac to get this boy out, and me as well.'

'No, Ken, you stay on the track for at least two more days. I'll evacuate all police personnel families to Jabiru. They can enjoy some quality time in the Crocodile Hotel at the Government's expense, under police guard. I'll also dispatch specialist officers to set up a trap for Ungara and Chicken George. What's your position, Ken? Jenkins and an ambulance officer can pick up the boy. The R44 is much faster than the Blackhawk. Leave someone with him and continue the hunt.'

'Chicken George is armed with the Glock, Ken,' Jack said. 'Ungara is traditional and has his club and spears. That means there are still two rifles with the mob. I reckon now that Ungara is gone, it won't be long before we catch up.'

The hunting party set off, the trackers loping easily ahead, following the tracks of the fugitives on the dusty plain. Oddly, it was Kangii who had offered to stay with the boy. He said that he would catch up as soon as the helicopter landed. It took them the rest of the day to reach the outlier on the vast plain. Beyond it, the escarpment rose into the cloudless sky.

Jack pointed to a gap. 'That's where the tracks are heading. Good spot for another ambush.'

Ken noted that the trackers hung back when they reached the gap. They started chanting and hitting their thighs with resounding slaps. Jack and Ken also joined in, shouting and clapping their hands loudly. A few minutes later they slowly entered the gorge, to be confronted by a large amphitheater where stone-lined paths ended at numerous caves that held hollow logs and paperbark rolls.

'Burial place,' Jack said in awe. 'There must be hundreds of bodies here. It looks like every cave and shelter has a coffin. No wonder the boys made all that noise to let the spirits know we were coming.'

'Never seen anything like it, certainly not as big as this one,' Ken replied. 'I've seen some smaller burial chambers, but this blows them out of the water. They must have laid the dead to rest here for hundreds, perhaps thousands, of years. And just look at those paintings. Amazing, it truly is. The boys are a bit worried; we'd better keep moving before they run away. I don't blame them one bit.

This place is spooky. Looks like our little bandits also thought so, they were running here. Not a place I want to spend the night in. I'm not superstitious, but this is something else.'

The men were more than happy to leave the dead and their spirits in peace behind them. As they neared the escarpment they noted that far to the north, masses of high clouds had built up – the first storm of the season. The heat was intense.

Toby had taken the lead, setting a cracking pace that would have killed lesser men; these were no ordinary men, though: they were hard bushmen, born and bred in the bush, who gave no thoughts about the hardships that would kill an urban dweller. The plain ended; once more they were back in open monsoon forest and stony ridge country that changed at every turn as, ahead, the escarpment loomed like a forbidden fortress wall.

Thunder moaned and rolled across the plain and forest before bouncing back from the high walls ahead. They now encountered more outliers separated by narrow ravines and running springs, where the hunting party shared cool spring water with thirsty birds that grudgingly fluttered out of their way. The storm was gathering pace and the light was failing when Toby pointed to a wall about twenty metres high, where a yawning hole offered sanctuary from the hostile elements.

The men entered a huge cave where a thousand fires had been burned by former occupants who had moved away a long time ago.

A rock wallaby suddenly bounced from the darkness, only to fall victim to a well-aimed rock tossed by David. Dinner was taken care of.

Inside the cave LED torches lit up partly burned timber, bones and dry branches that covered wooden sleeping platforms. The droppings of rock wallabies and rats indicated that they had occupied the cave after man had abandoned it. It was also full of mosquitoes who gave them an unexpected and rather unwanted welcome. The men stopped slapping themselves after smoky leaf fires finally drove the biting nuisances out into the darkness.

Tracker Joey pointed to where a white ochre figure was painted on the wall: a woman, her hands above her head, a streaky white line hovering over her.

'Lighting woman place,' Joey said in a strange tone. 'Long time that woman bin hit by lighting from big storm and die in this place. Maybe not good place to stay.'

'Don't worry, Joey,' Ken replied. 'That lightning only hit in one place once. Fuck, that was close,' he added as lighting crackled outside followed by a thunderous crash that rattled the cave walls.

Outside, the tempest ruled, fire and lighting lit up the land as Namarrkun the lighting man, bounced his stone axes from the earth and the clouds. They cracked off rocks on the escarpment and hit tall trees, splintering them to match wood.

Flame and blinding white light lit up the cave opening as streaks of lightning bolts flashed and hit trees nearby, followed by a rumbling explosion that almost deafened the men. They had to shout to make themselves heard, getting courage from each other's company as the storm roared on.

Ken had lit a cooking fire, the flames casting ghostly shadows upon the walls; the rock art frieze appeared alive with ghostly dreamtime figures. The men gathered about the fire, talking loudly to make themselves heard above the tumultuous thunder and, more importantly, to scare off the spirits that were all about them. The small rock wallaby was tossed on the fire, the smell of burning hair soon making room for the smell of cooked meat. They cut away tasty bits with their knives and chewed on it until an uncooked section was found. It was tossed back on the coals to cook properly while another piece was cut from the animal.

'I wonder why Kangii has not caught up with us,' Ken mused. 'The chopper must have been late.'

'No, Ken,' Toby replied. 'He told me that he will be tracking Ungara and Chicken George. He swore me to secrecy. He told me not to worry about your family, he'll look after them.'

Daylight was still a promise when Jack, who had been on watch, woke the men.

The cave was dark with the coals of the fire giving off only a faint glow. Breakfast was a hot mug of tea. The men headed out of the cave into the forest, the earth smelling fresh and clean as if reborn after the storm.

14

PARADISE

Ahead, a high, impregnable wall extended into the heavens above them. The rain had washed out the tracks of the fugitives and their only hope was to come across them again. Toby pointed to a crack in the wall to their right.

'That looks like a ravine. We need to get closer to make sure.'

It was a beautiful, sunny day with only fleecy clouds towards the north. The scent of the forest was in the air, fresh and invigorating. The crack slowly opened to a narrow chasm. A shallow pool below a small trickling waterfall lay at its entrance. Tracks indicated that the fugitives had been digging for mussels hours earlier. The smoldering remains of a fire and cracked shells lay nearby. The men were elated; once more they followed the tracks like blood hounds.

The narrow ravine opened to a wide-spread verdant valley that extended far to the south, the high escarpment walls rising high above patches of monsoon rainforests and open woodland. The men stood on a high ledge that overlooked a mosaic of green – fig, paperbark, and palm trees.

'Bloody hell,' Ken exclaimed. 'This is a hidden world, a paradise. I've never seen anything like it.'

'I have, mate,' Jack replied. 'There are a couple of gorges like this in the southern stone country. But they've long been forgotten by the current people. Most of the old people who can still remember living in the stone country as children are gone. The modern generation prefer parties and getting drunk instead of exploring and camping. They have no clue on what they're missing out on.'

The men entered the rain forest, a twilight zone: cool, but humid compared to the lowlands. The crystal-clear water of the spring-fed creek was alive with small fish, turtles, and freshwater crocodiles hidden in the shadows under the forest canopy. Crimson finches and honey eaters chattered loudly at the intruders as they followed them and fluttered about in pandanus fronds. A thick carpet of leaves, still wet from the rain, dampened their footsteps. The tracks of the fugitives were well indicated by the upturned leaves and in sandy places. They appeared to be in no hurry as no attempts were made to hide them.

'They bin think that we bin lost them,' David remarked. 'Not long now we catch up.'

By midday the humidity became unbearable. The hunt was forgotten as the men, naked, plunged into a small rock pool, the water cool and invigorating. The crocodiles, fish, and turtles grudgingly gave way. The trackers caught three turtles and tossed them onto the bank. Nono was in the process of lighting a cooking fire when he stopped and sniffed the air.

'That mob close by,' Nono whispered. 'That smell from cooking fire. I reckon we sneak up and catch them now.'

The men gathered up their weapons and stalked towards the smoke smell. They were on edge, every footstep measured and planned to avoid stepping on a stick or a dry leaf. Some 400 metres later they reached a grove of tall trees. Smoke lazily curled from it. The men used tree trunks and bushes as cover. There was no need for signals; every hunter knew his job. Ken had given strict instructions not to shoot unless they were fired upon.

Closer they stalked, following the smell of the cooked turtle meat. The forest was dense, its canopy blocking out the sun. Dappled shadows hid their approach. Jack, on the outside, signaled for the nearest trackers to encircle the still invisible camp. The men closed in, crouching low; their eyes were eager, their breath deep with suppressed excitement; adrenalin coursed in their blood, thrumming through fingers on triggers. They were invisible in the dappling shadows. Ahead were the fugitives, completely at ease, happy in the knowledge that their pursuers had given up. The girls were sitting together, apart from one prodding the fire with a stick. The boys were sitting on the trunk of a palm tree, chattering happy. Suddenly the camp was invaded by yelling armed men. The girls screamed in fear and tried to flee, but they were herded back with harsh orders by the police party. A boy made a grab for a rifle. He fumbles with it, trying to get the safety catch off. A rifle butt smashed into his wooly skull. Another grabbed a spear, but Ken hit him across his face with his rifle barrel.

Nono yelled loudly at the girls to stop screaming, telling them they are safe and have nothing to fear. Two girls recognized Nono and ran over, crying loudly, tears streaming down their face. Nono called at the others to sit down and not run away. The girls hugged Nono as if they would never let him go. The hunt was over.

The boys, their hands cuffed with cable ties behind their backs, were silent; the fight had gone out from them. They told a tale of intimidation, fear and murder, under the leadership of Ungara. No one had dared to challenge him, or his lieutenant, Chicken George. They told the police that Ungara and Chicken George had become best friends who had sworn to kill all Balanders from Arnhem Land. All during the dry season they had hidden in the Arufura Swamp, always on the move when the searchers came close. Only when the dry season ended did they break free from the mosquitoes and crocodiles.

Ungara had told them of a place in the stone

country where no one would find them. He said he would bring more girls after killing all the hated whites in Arnhem Land.

Ken, unable to get a signal on the sat phone or find an open space for the helicopter to land, gathered his men and prisoners and turned back to the open country beyond the escarpment. It was almost mid-afternoon when they left the narrow chasm and rested in a shady place near the plunge pool. Ken got a clear signal and called Fields.

'It's over, Peter. We have the boys and girls. No one is badly hurt. Can you get us out of here ASAP? We don't fancy another night in a cave being bombarded by lightning and thunder if another storm builds up, though it appears unlikely now.'

'No worries at all. I'll have the army pick up the prisoners and take them to Darwin. We need to know their true story, and of course the girls will need to be checked to make sure they are healthy and well. Anyway, I have to run and get your people home if I can get two more helicopters. Nono, Jack, and his boys also need to get home. The army can drop you and Toby off at Jabiru. They'll have to refuel there. It'll give you a chance to catch up with your family and have a day off.'

15

EXECUTION

Ken was back in his office, looking across the plain; it was scattered with a hint of greening after a storm had dropped a little rain some days earlier. Beyond the plain, the outlier rose tall above a shimmering mirage, as if it was standing on a shaky platform; it was a familiar and comforting scene. Inspector Field, Toby, and Senior Sergeant Andy Divine, in charge of the Rapid Response Team, were also in the room.

'Ken, it's been six days now since Ungara and Chicken George left their mob. They should be here by now, but there have been no sightings or tracks at all. With luck, Kangii caught up and did the job for us. That would be a preferred outcome for everyone.'

'I have my men well hidden,' Divine, a big broad-shouldered man, said in his lazy drawling voice. 'They are well armed, and I have several snipers looking for any sign of the fugitives. Patrols armed with night vision roam about the perimeter at night. According to your own reports, Ken, Ungara likes to operate during a full moon when his spirits are with him. Well, that's tonight. My men are well prepared.'

Suddenly Toby jumped up and pointed to where three puffs of black smoke rose above the escarpment outlier into the cloudless, almost white sky of the dry season heat.

'Kangii,' Toby uttered. 'He told me that he would send a signal if Ungara was close. Ungara is on that hill, waiting to strike tonight.'

'The bush telegraph is alive and well,' Ken exclaimed. 'I knew that Kangii wouldn't let us down.'

'But doesn't he have a contract on Ungara?' Irvine asked.

'He does, but not on Chicken George,' Ken replied. 'It would be wrong for him to kill him, so he's letting us have him. He'll also be wary going up against two armed men and needs our help. Plus, it matters little to him if we kill Ungara also, as long as the job is done one way or another.'

'Bloody blackfella politics,' Fields groaned. 'We Balanders will never get the gist of it. Not as long as I live anyway. What now, Ken?'

'Well, if we all rush up at once, there's a huge chance that our targets will slip away into the main escarpment,' Ken replied, pointing to a wall map. 'The Central Arnhem Road separates them from escape. The hill is only a small stand-alone outlier, but it's full of caves and shelters. They can hide in there forever if they want to, apart from getting hungry. But there's no game and only a little spring for water. We have enough men to cut him off from his planned sanctuary.

The whole area has been burned so there is no cover to hide in, and nowhere to run. There's about 200 metres of relatively open ground between the outlier and the main complex, including the fifty-metre-wide road. Put snipers in the rocks along the road and they can take anyone out who crosses the road, even at night with night vision. But for Christ's sake, make sure they don't shoot Kangii. In the meantime, Toby and I will hunt the men and hopefully link up with Kangii.'

'That's bloody risky, Ken,' Fields said, concern in his voice. 'I'm not sure I want you or Toby to even consider it.'

'Only way, Peter. We've spent long weeks in the field tracking the bastard and know him very well. With luck, he has no clue that we even know he's up there. Kangii's smoke signal only lasted for a few seconds and there's no doubt that Ungara and Chicken George's attention is directed towards us, not behind them. Toby and I will head out when it cools down a bit. Andy can get his men discreetly in position. I suggest that he has at least two men in each squad, so they can look after each other in case Ungara stalks them. You game, Toby?'

'Mah, it's my job, or have you forgotten what he did to my family last year?'

'No offense meant, mate, but I thought I'd better ask first. Let's get our gear and weapons ready. I suggest you take one of the slide-action shotguns and load it with buckshot. I know that I will, and my trusty .357 Magnum as well.'

Thunder was moaning to the northeast when Divine dropped Ken and Toby off where the hill commenced from the road. The two men headed for the outlier, sweating profusely in the intense humidly. The land was breathless; there was no movement, no wind, no birds, nothing; the silence was absolute, even the ever-present crow carks absent. Only a pair of wedge-tailed eagles floated high in the heavens on an invisible uplift. The men reached the first of the rocks and followed a game path to the top of the ridge where huge sandstone rocks littered the area.

Toby led, armed with a twelve-gauge Winchester short-barreled shotgun. It was loaded with six rounds of buckshot, each round containing nine lead balls designed for maximum destruction on flesh – human or game. He also carried his police issue 10mm Glock. Ken had a similar shotgun, and was armed with his .357 Magnum S&W double-action revolver.

The outlier was a labyrinth of rocks and thorny scrubs that tore at their clothing as if trying to restrain the hunters. They crawled on hands and knees under the prickly bushes and rock falls where rocks were perched precariously on top of each other. Toby knew the hill well; he had been there many times, playing hide and seek as a small child. Later, as he got older, he hunted rock wallabies during the wet season when the hill had both grass and water. But now, it was dry and austere.

Suddenly Toby paused, his heart skipping a beat. He pointed to the ground, where the dust revealed three sets of footprints. 'Ungara, Chicken George, and Kangii,' Toby whispered to Ken. 'Kangii is tracking them. Not far now.'

He put his finger on his lips to indicate for Ken to use the utmost silence. They had gone no more than thirty metres when Toby lost the tracks on a large slab of bare rock. Ahead was an imposing jumble of tall rocks, from where the plain stretched to Balanya. This was Toby's backyard; he was in charge. Ken was more than happy to follow his directions. He had complete trust in him.

Toby waved to Ken to take the right turn about the rock pile as he took the left. The sun had vanished behind a huge storm far to the west. Ken became acutely aware that thunder was rumbling from another storm over the nearby escarpment. It would be upon them soon. He suddenly paused alongside a large rock, bringing the shotgun to battery as something moved ahead. But it was a spotted nightjar, roosting on a small ledge under an overhang.

Ken relaxed and dropped the barrel down, just as something whizzed past his head and slammed into the rock. Rapid gunfire broke the silence. Bullets slammed all about Ken, ricocheting from the rocks, the exploding rock splinters and bullet fragments showering his face and back. A sliver hit him above his eyes, the blood blinding him. Ken spun about and fired at a blurred figure no more than ten metres away. There was a shrill cry of pain. Ken racked the slide back and fired again. Another shot hit the rock behind him, driving more slivers of razor-sharp rock into his back. Ken fired once more, his eyes clouded with blood. There was no return fire.

Ken wiped his shirt sleeve across his eyes, but it failed to clear his vision. He placed the shotgun against the rock, pulled his shirt up, and wiped his forehead with it. It partly cleared his eyes. His blurred vision revealed Chicken George lying against a rock, still clinging to the stolen pistol, his life blood pumping from eighteen holes in his bare chest.

Suddenly there was a cry of pure hate. Someone leaped from the rock from behind the dead boy – Ungara, his woomera loaded with a deadly spear. Ken made a desperate grab for the shotgun, still partly blinded from the bleeding wound on his forehead. In his mind he knew that he was too late and too slow. He braced for the spear's impact as he gripped the front of the gun, racked the slide, brought the shotgun to battery, and fired. He knew that he had missed.

Something whizzed above Ken with great speed and slammed into Ungara's chest with a loud resounding thud. He dropped his spear and woomera with a loud tortured scream of pain and stumbled forward, clutching at a spear sticking out of his chest. It had neatly parted his breastbone. Ungara fell onto the rocks, the blood pouring from the fatal wound joining that of his lieutenant. Ungara was dead, the hunt was over. He was only days away from his twentieth birthday.

Ken slumped down on his haunches. Kangii was suddenly in front of him, grabbing his shoulder. He spoke in a calm voice, and while Ken did not understand a word of it, he knew what he was saying. He grabbed Kangii's arm for support and stood up.

'Not sure what you're saying, Kangii, but I reckon I know what you're talking about. You saved my life and I can never repay you for what you did, or for the help that you gave us.'

Toby was suddenly there. Ken always marveled how he and Kangii could be so silent. Both men were of the same mould and had become the best of friends since their first meeting. Toby spoke for Ken, his words meeting with a nod of approval. Kangii gripped Ken's shoulder with a firm hand and said something before turning about and holding Toby by the shoulder for a moment. He walked away into what Ken thought was a void, though he later said that it must have been his still blurred vision. He heard Toby's voice; it sounded far away.

'Kangii says that his work is done. He considers us his best friends and wishes us well in the lands of the Balander. He also said that you have big balls – and if you ever want his help, you should walk into the bush and call him. He will come …'

About the author

Dick Eussen has lived in the Australian tropics since 1959, where he has spent a lifetime working in the bush, on cattle stations, and living in remote mining communities. He also owned and operated a tour operation out of Port Douglas into the Daintree Rainforest for over a decade. He is Australia's premier and one of the most published freelance outdoor writer/photographers in the country. His first magazine piece was published in 1957. He currently freelances for a dozen magazines and submits articles and photographs to photography, fishing, hunting and shooting, camping, 4WD, boating and quad bike adventures, bush lore, and northern history to national magazines. He is the author of seven factual books on fishing, hunting and camping along the Savannah Way – Cairns to Broome. Dick and his wife Eileen live at Mareeba from where they take regular bush trips to ensure that his many readers are kept informed on the tropical lifestyle when they head north.